ACROSS
THE DIVIDE

Other Catnip titles by Anne Booth

Girl With a White Dog
Dog Ears

ACROSS THE DIVIDE

Anne Booth

Catnip
PUBLISHING LTD

CATNIP BOOKS
Published by Catnip Publishing Ltd
320 City Road
London EC1V 2NZ
www.catnippublishing.co.uk

This edition first published 2018

1 3 5 7 9 10 8 6 4 2

ISBN 978-1-91061-1111

Printed and bound by CPI Group (UK) Ltd, Croydon, CR0 4YY

To Peace-makers and Peace-keepers

throughout the world

'*Not to speak is to speak. Not to act is to act.*'

Dietrich Bonhoeffer

'*We have far more in common with each other than things that divide us.*'

Jo Cox, MP

Chapter One

The only thing I was absolutely sure about at the beginning of the holiday was that I didn't want to go to Lindisfarne. I wasn't sure what to do about all the arguments at school – and especially about what was happening with Aidan – but I did know that I didn't want to spend summer half-term with Dad, miles away on an island.

Before everything went wrong, I'd had lots of things planned for the holiday. Not that those plans would have worked out exactly, after all that had happened in the weeks leading up to half-term, but that wasn't the point.

The point was that even when I did have an opinion, it didn't count. So what was the point in saying what I thought about anything? Nobody would listen to me anyway. For example, I didn't think it was a good idea for Mum to go on the demonstration in the first place – I even asked her not to – and what happened? She went and got arrested, that's what. On the first day of my holiday.

If Gran and Grandad had been at home there wouldn't have been a problem. And I didn't understand why they had suddenly decided to go on holiday at half-term. Without me. They had only just agreed to let me come back and live with them at the vicarage. They knew I couldn't stay at home alone, and that if they weren't there I would have to go back to Mum's. They had never mentioned wanting to go on a cruise before, only that this was a last-minute bargain, which Gran said was too good to miss.

Still, it would have been all right if Mum had been responsible. I could just about have coped with staying with her for half-term week. It might even have been nice. Maybe a miracle would have happened and we could have talked about what was going on at school. Like we used to. Maybe Mum would have actually listened to me for once and we could have sorted things out between us. I could have gone and met my friends in town and had a quiet time at home with Mum, like a normal family. We could have watched films when she came back from work, we could have relaxed. Like before.

Before she got all involved with her pacifist friends and started arguing with everyone.

It was Mum who messed everything up. Mum and Johnny knew I didn't want Mum to go on a protest on Saturday, my first day back with her, because I told them so. Not that I should have had to do that. It was pretty obvious that if your daughter moves back with you on the Friday evening, and if you have been missing her, you shouldn't rush off first thing Saturday morning.

I thought Johnny would support me, but he didn't. All he cared about was being a good boyfriend to Mum – which, as far as I could see, basically meant agreeing with everything she did. He said the protest was a good thing to do and if he wasn't busy sorting some things out for a family thing that weekend, he would have gone. He said I shouldn't give my mum a hard time.

'Have a lie-in, Olivia. Chill out a bit. It's just for the morning,' he said. Typical Johnny.

When Mum was leaving she said she was only going to watch and to support the other protesters, but someone got ill at the last minute so Mum took his place and took part herself. So she got arrested. I wasn't impressed. Nobody else had a mum who got arrested for cutting holes in a military fence and weaving flowers through it.

So I had to go to stay with Dad. But that wasn't simple either. Dad lived miles away, in Durham, but he was having building work done on his house, which was why he was renting a place on the island of Lindisfarne for a few months while he wrote a book. Apparently it was the perfect place for his research. So that was that. Lindisfarne it was, whether I liked it or not.

She did apologize.

'I'm so sorry, Olivia,' Mum said on the phone Johnny had handed me. He had come to ours from his flat downstairs, as soon as Mum rang him. 'It's taken me by surprise. They say I have to stay in police custody until I go before the court on Monday morning.'

'You're staying in a police cell all weekend?' I couldn't believe it. We hadn't even had our first lunch together and Mum was locked up.

Mum's voice shook a little, which made me feel a bit funny. 'Yes. And . . . I'm sure this isn't going to happen, so don't get cross, but there's a slight – a slight – possibility we will be transferred to prison and have to stay there for the weeks before the trial . . .'

'Weeks!' I said.

'It probably won't happen. I'm sure I will be back on Monday. Don't freak out, Olivia. I'm sorry, but you need to pack quickly. Johnny's been amazing. He's arranging everything. He phoned your dad to let him know that I was arrested and won't be able to come home for a few days. Johnny will buy the train ticket and take you to the station on his way to his mum's. He will put you on the train to Berwick. Your father will meet you there and you can go to Lindisfarne with him.'

'But Mum,' I said. 'I don't want to go to Lindisfarne. Northumberland is miles away. Can't I just stay here with someone else until Gran and Grandad come home?'

'Look, Olivia,' said Mum. 'I'm sorry. Hopefully I should be given bail on Monday and then I will be released. I just need you to go to your dad's this weekend because I know from something Sister Mary has said that I can't absolutely guarantee that. Johnny won't be here, your gran and grandad aren't around and I can't ask some other family to put you up if I don't know when I will be out – I don't even know how long it will be for. It's better if you go to your dad's. Just for the weekend. It will be fun. Lindisfarne is beautiful. You'll love it.'

'Well, thanks a lot, Mum,' I said sarcastically.

I did feel a bit sorry for her, because her voice was a bit wobbly, but I was mainly cross. Gran had gone on and on about how much she was sure Mum was missing me and wanted me to come back to live with her in the flat, but Gran was obviously wrong. Mum had had the chance to spend half-term with me, her own daughter, and she had blown it. All Mum cared about was her peace work. I wasn't impressed. What good was going on marches and signing petitions and putting flowers in fences and singing songs about peace, anyway? How did that stop wars?

Mum messed up. I think that's what I want to say. I knew Gran was worried about what had happened only a few weeks before, at the start of May, and that Mum was hurt when I walked out and moved back to the vicarage. Maybe she was. But I had to do it. It wasn't just because of the row we had about me wanting to join the cadets, either. Gran had no idea how annoying it was, living with Mum in that flat. Like when our already tiny front room was taken over by people making banners and stuff for the next peace demonstration. I'd had enough of piles of envelopes on the table, waiting to be stuffed with leaflets, and someone I didn't know sitting on our sofa and using our laptop to check facts or post things on the campaign's Facebook page or whatever else they did. I was fed up of unwashed coffee mugs everywhere, and the kitchen being so full of people arguing about the government I couldn't get to the kettle to make myself a cup of tea – and how if I did, Johnny would say, 'Oh, great idea! Put the kettle on, Olivia. Now, who's for tea and who's for coffee?'

I knew Grandad would be angry about her getting arrested. He understood what I meant. You could talk to him about things. He said she was really irresponsible, protesting all the time. I told him that if Mum wanted to do things that are against the law that was her decision. It wasn't mine. I was fourteen. I was old enough to know what I wanted to do, who I wanted to live with.

And how I wanted to spend my holiday. If I had a choice.

Dad and I could see the castle from miles away. I was still really fed up, but I had to admit to myself that it looked dramatic up on the hill, silhouetted against the skyline. We turned off at a place called Beal, waited at the level crossing before driving past a farm and a birds of prey centre, and then we were on the causeway, past the sign saying: *Danger! Holy Island causeway. Look at the tide tables*. The tide tables themselves were there too, and a warning to only cross when the tide is out. It wasn't exactly encouraging, all these warning signs. And why had the place got two names, anyway – Lindisfarne *and* Holy Island?

It was odd how the wet sand between us and the island, normally underwater, was at the same level as the road, so it felt like crossing through the sea. A bit like that Bible story about Moses which Grandad used to tell me. There was sand on either side of us, but the sea was not far away, waiting to cross the divide and reclaim the land between as soon as the time was right.

'So what would happen if we crossed at the wrong time? When the tide was coming in?' I asked, without really thinking it through.

Dad turned his head and raised an eyebrow sarcastically.

'In answer to your question,' he said, 'if we tried to break the rules, and crossed outside the safe times, then we could get stranded. That's why there are those towers every so often along the causeway – they're for people who thought they could beat the sea. You can't cross over at the wrong time. If you misjudge it, or ignore the warnings, you can take refuge in the towers until the tide goes out or a person in a boat comes to rescue you. But if you have to leave your car on the road and the tide comes in, then your car will be wrecked. And you will only have yourself to blame. I can't believe how many people ignore the warnings and don't learn from other people's mistakes. Crossing from one side to the other is dangerous. You can't take risks. It's so irresponsible. You have to be careful.'

Even the way he changed gear was irritated. He wasn't normally like this. I didn't like it.

'OK, I'm not an idiot,' I muttered under my breath. 'I didn't need a lecture or have my head bitten off.'

Dad gave a short, impatient sigh. 'Sorry, Olivia. I'm just cross with your mum. Look, neither of us really want you to be here, but we're just going to have to put up with each other.'

That hurt. But I was determined not to show him it did.

'Don't worry, I'll keep well out of your way. You won't even know I'm here,' I snapped.

There was a pause.

'I'm sorry,' said Dad. 'It's just . . . It's just all a bit sudden and I have a deadline to meet. I booked this house so I could have some peace and quiet to get on with my work, and get the extension finished at home, and . . . this . . . you . . . just wasn't – weren't – in my plan. OK?'

'It wasn't exactly in my plan, either,' I said, staring out of the window. I could see some birds in the distance picking their way across it. Sandpipers, or curlews perhaps. I sighed and my breath misted up the window. Aidan would know. But he was hardly someone I could talk to any more. Not now. Whether I was in Lindisfarne or not.

'Olivia . . . Look, I'm sorry.'

I felt tears prick behind my eyes, which really annoyed me. 'I'm not just pieces you have to pick up. I'm your daughter,' I said.

'I know. And I'm sorry. It's fine, honestly. I'm just feeling a bit stressed. Forgive me? I truly am sorry. It's good we can spend some time together. I do want to. Of course I do. This is important to me. *You're* important to me. Forgive me?'

I heard the thumping of a tail in the back. Stan had woken up and decided to join the conversation. The red setter's head pushed its way between us and he gave my nose an enthusiastic lick.

'Go back and lie down, Stan,' said Dad. Stan obediently retreated, but you could still hear him panting with excitement, and the happy sound of his tail hitting the back seat. He gave an enthusiastic woof, and Dad and I looked at each other and laughed. It was hard to stay cross when Stan was about. He loved everyone so much, all the time.

'OK,' I said, as sand dunes appeared and we drove off the causeway and on to the island.

'Great,' said Dad. 'It'll all be OK – honestly, Olivia.'

Stan had lifted my mood. I'd be home on Monday, and this wasn't a bad place to visit for the weekend. It was beautiful, and it would be fun to be with Stan anyway. I looked up to see the castle looking down on us, and had the strangest feeling that it was glad I had come.

Chapter Two

I hadn't wanted to leave Gran and Grandad in the first place. It was back in Year Six, and the vicarage was the only home I had ever known. We'd been living with them since I was born. Before it, actually. Mum was only sixteen and Dad was seventeen when she got pregnant. She came to live with Dad at Gran and Grandad's, and it was fine. We were happy.

Mum was lucky. Grandad isn't like a very old man or anything. Nor is he just a vicar – he's a major in the army reserves, and served in Afghanistan. And Gran is really fun, as well as kind and gentle. She does loads of stuff, like salsa dancing and painting and pottery, and makes Grandad laugh. Gran used to laugh a lot with Mum too.

The vicarage is big, so there was plenty of room for us all. Dad left for university in Durham when I was a baby and only came back for visits, but

Gran and Grandad were really helpful and looked after me so that Mum could go off to college and study to be a gardener. Mum loves flowers. Grandad always said she has 'green fingers'. Gran and Grandad even bought her a van and put her name on it and everything. They really looked after her and loved her, even though she wasn't their daughter.

They did everything for us, for me and Mum and Dad.

It was Mum who chose to break that up and move into the flat – and take me with her.

It started with the poppies.

Nobody else I knew made such a fuss about red poppies. People bought them to raise money for the British Legion, and to remember all the soldiers who died in the war. Red poppies were in loads of poems because they grew on the battlefields in the First World War. So I thought it was just ridiculous of Mum to get so cross about them.

I remember that the argument was at breakfast time. I came down with my uniform on. Mum was eating toast. Gran was washing up.

'Olivia,' said Mum. 'Why are you wearing a red poppy?'

'Because it's the Remembrance service today,'

I said. 'We're all walking down to the church and Grandad is going to take the service.'

'But where did you get the poppy from?' Mum said.

'They sold them at school,' I said.

'You didn't ask me for any money for it,' said Mum. 'I normally give you the money for school things.'

'Oh, I gave her a pound,' said Gran.

Mum tutted. I wondered why Gran giving me a pound had annoyed her so much.

Gran stopped washing up and looked round.

'Sorry, Caz, have I done something wrong?'

'I just would have appreciated it if I had been told what was going on in my own daughter's school,' Mum said.

I remember feeling she wasn't being very fair to Gran. I *had* told Mum about the Remembrance service – parents were welcome – but she'd said she couldn't come because she had work. I figured she must have a headache or something, and that she would apologize in a few minutes. That's what Mum is like – she flares up but she's always quick to say sorry. She and Gran never normally argued. Mum and Grandad argued loads, but it was never nasty.

They argued mainly about gardening – about the best way to grow carrots or how to get rid of slugs – but they could argue about anything really, from how to make biscuits to who knew the most answers on *University Challenge* or whose curry recipe was best. But it was a comfortable way of arguing. They were happy. Not like this.

'Nothing's "going on" – it's just Remembrance Day,' I said, pouring some cereal into a bowl. I poured the milk on and, out of habit, tried to hear the popping sound of the rice, but Mum was talking over it, her voice getting louder and louder.

'Were they selling white poppies too?' Mum asked.

'No,' I said, and shrugged. 'What's the point of white poppies? They're not red like blood. That's why we have the red ones.'

'I just can't believe this!' said Mum.

'What can't you believe?' said Grandad, coming into the kitchen.

'That clearly no one at the school talked to the children about white poppies. People like you have imposed your views on them and not even bothered to talk about alternatives to this glorification of war,' Mum snapped.

I remember Grandad's face changing. I looked over at Gran – we both knew Mum had gone too far.

'I don't glorify war, Caz. I've seen what it does. I honour those who gave their lives for this country and I'm not ashamed of it.' His voice was quiet but very angry.

Mum should have left it there. But she didn't.

'I'm sorry, Andrew, but I think it's outrageous that the children have been encouraged to buy red poppies but nobody has sold white ones for peace.'

'Well, it's not too late,' said Gran. I think she was trying to be helpful. 'Where would we get these white poppies?'

'It *is* too late, Ruth. The service is today. We can figure it out for next year,' said Grandad.

'No, I think it's a good idea. Thank you,' said Mum to Gran, and she just got up and walked out.

'What on earth was that all about?' said Grandad.

'I think she's finding things a bit difficult, that's all,' said Gran, shooting Grandad a look. 'I think communication in this house could be bit better, to be honest. Acceptance of different views . . .'

'That's hardly fair!' said Grandad, humphing a bit as he left the kitchen.

Gran sighed.

'What's happening?' I said. 'Why is Mum having a difficult time?'

Gran dried her hands on a towel and opened her arms for a hug. 'There's nothing to worry about, Olivia,' she said, as I pressed against her.

But there was.

When we walked down the road to the church that morning, I could see Mum at the doorway with a cardboard box in her hand.

'There's your mum!' said Riya, who was walking next to me, and waved at her. 'That's nice.' Riya has always really liked Mum. She enjoyed being in the junior-school gardening club that Mum ran after school, and said Mum was really kind and good at teaching them about plants. Riya thinks she is exciting – I reckon it's Mum's pink hair and nose stud. It's funny, because me and Riya are the only girls I know whose mums both have nose studs, but Riya's mum stays at home with Riya's little brothers and sisters. She doesn't do any campaigning or argue with anyone or try to save the world. Lucky Riya.

I saw Mum try to give something to Mrs Harper, the Head, and Mrs Harper shake her head and say something. Then I saw Mrs Harper stand next to Mum and wave everyone past. Mum darted forward to give something white to someone in Year Five, and Mrs Harper put her hand on Mum's arm.

All the time, our form were getting nearer and nearer.

'What's up with your mum, Olivia?' said Nola, just behind me.

I remember my face getting all hot.

Then I saw Grandad come out, in his vestments, and talk to Mum and wave his arms at her.

Then Gran came out and put her arm around Mum, and Mum threw it off and stormed off down the path away from us.

'Oh, your mum doesn't seem to be staying after all,' said Riya, sounding disappointed.

But I was glad. I didn't understand what had happened, but I was glad it was over.

But the problem was that it wasn't over.

We had the service. We sang 'Jerusalem', which is Grandad's favourite hymn, and we had a minute's silence for all the soldiers who had died. When we got back, we played netball and I scored three goals. Later, one of my drawings got put on the wall – it was a poster of a soldier with a poppy. I remember colouring it in red and Riya seeing it.

'You're so brilliant at art,' she said. 'The red

poppies look great. Why was your mum trying to give us white poppies?'

I remember shrugging and saying, 'I don't know,' but thinking that I was not looking forward to going home to see Mum arguing with Grandad.

But I didn't even have to wait until then to see Mum arguing. She was outside the school gate at the end of the day and she had that box of white poppies again. This time she was arguing with Nola's uncle. Nola and Eddie didn't have a mum and dad – they lived with their uncle and aunt. They are both lovely and Mum's known them for years.

'It's not appropriate, Caz,' he was saying. 'We've got Nola's brother in Afghanistan on active service at the moment. Our boys need solidarity now, not this.'

'It's not against soldiers, Bill, it's against war,' said Mum. 'It's to their benefit – they don't have to be killed if there are no wars.'

Nola's uncle saw Nola and I coming over.

'Who has been killed?' Nola said. 'Is Eddie OK?'

'Nobody, Nola. Don't worry,' said her uncle Bill. 'Eddie is fine. For Pete's sake, Caz, stop talking about soldiers being killed. This is an army town. You're just going to upset people.'

Then it got really nasty, because Tyler Lambert's

dad heard what was going on. He strode over, took the box of white poppies from Mum and threw them on the ground. Emily Reed's mum saw and started yelling at Mum to show some respect and leave everyone alone. Mum was trying to pick up the white poppies, and crying a bit. Nola and I went to help pick them up and Nola's uncle told them both to calm down. And they did, although they joined a group of other parents and I could hear them saying, 'Cheek!' and 'What does she think she's doing?' and 'Our lads are putting their lives at risk for her.' It was horrible.

'Thanks, Olivia, Nola,' said Mum. Her hands were shaking. 'That wasn't very nice, was it? I'm sorry if you got worried, Nola. I'm sure nothing will happen to Eddie.'

Which was a bit of a lie – even if it was, as Gran would say, a white one. Mum wasn't sure. Nobody was. He was fighting in a war. Mum often said to me she was worried about him being in Afghanistan. Mum was very fond of Eddie. He used to be in her gardening club when she first started it, and he grew the tallest sunflower that year. Mum said he was so proud. She took a photograph of him. We still have a copy. He looked so sweet, so small next to the flower.

'Caz? Olivia? Come with Nola and me – I'll give you a lift home,' said Nola's uncle. He put his arm across Mum's shoulders and gave her a quick hug, and walked us over to his car. Nobody bothered us, because he was there. Bill used to be in the army, and lost his leg in an explosion in Northern Ireland.

'Why do you always do these things?' he said to Mum when we got in the car. 'Why do you look for trouble, Caz?'

'I'm just trying to make the world better for our children,' said Mum.

I remember how Bill sighed. 'I know,' he said.

But I was her child, and I didn't see how making everyone look at me – and spoiling Remembrance Day – was making things better for me.

Chapter Three

Despite feeling fed up, I could still see that Lindisfarne was beautiful. *Really* beautiful. The old stone castle on the hill was like something from the telly or a postcard, and it was framed in my new bedroom window. We had crossed the causeway with an hour to spare, and once the sea was in, that was it. No way of running away until the tide changed again. Unless you had a boat. Which I hadn't.

Out of the window to the left, there were fields with sheep, and then, sloping down to the right, the beach and the sea. Over all of this was the sky – blue with smears of white cloud, and birds. Birds up in the air, and birds as I looked down on to the little garden directly under my window. Birds squabbling excitedly in the hedges and hopping about on the path. Not seagulls but sparrows. It was sort of nice to see them. They reminded me of home.

Sparrows. I'd never thought of them living by the sea. Maybe I'd get my sketchbook and draw them. Aidan always said I was good at drawing birds. I could send the picture to Mum. My stomach lurched as I wondered if I'd have to send it to a prison.

It made me feel horrible to think about Mum.

It made me feel horrible to think about Aidan.

But it wasn't my fault. About either of them.

'OK?' said Dad, standing in the doorway. 'All unpacked?'

I nodded. My clothes were in the drawers and hung up in the wardrobe. My suitcase was stowed under the bed, and my MP3 player, sketchbook and pencils were on the desk. I like things neat.

'I've rung Johnny. Your mum's OK but we won't know anything more about what's going to happen until Monday . . . And he said he'd ring and let us know when he does hear anything. You're not to worry. OK?'

I nodded again. I knew Mum was safe. Our country isn't one of those countries where people get killed for disagreeing with the government. And I knew Mum was with a nun – Sister Mary, who was eighty and had been a peace campaigner for years. I was sure there were lots of people who were trying to help get them released. I knew those things, but it still didn't feel right, being miles away, cut off by the tide. I bit my lip and blinked to stop the hot tears welling up. I didn't want to cry.

'I don't imagine you have much money with you?' Dad said.

I shook my head.

'Right. Well, I have got to work. I have a conference paper and a book to write,' he continued, almost as if talking to himself as much as to me. 'Just in case the worst comes to the worst and you have to stay here for a while, I think it's only fair that I give you a basic allowance. So you can buy yourself a hot chocolate in one of the cafes, or a book or something. Here's something to start it off.' He took out his wallet from his back pocket and handed me a twenty-pound note.

Twenty whole pounds? *Basic* allowance? Other people had that sort of pocket money, but Mum didn't earn much as a gardener, and so I just never expected any. Sometimes I did babysitting for her friends, but they didn't tend to have much money either. And now I had some finally, when I was miles away from home – so I could drink hot chocolate on my own, somewhere I didn't want to be. Typical.

'I'll go to Berwick or Alnwick for shopping,' Dad continued, 'so perhaps we can see if you could join the library there. Do you still like art?'

'Yes. You know that. You gave me a set of watercolours at Christmas.'

'I know. I just remember things changing a lot when I was your age. People change. I didn't want to take anything for granted.'

'Well, I do still like art,' I said. 'I'm going to do it for GCSE next year. I told you.'

'Yes. Of course. Sorry. So, that's good. Have you brought any art things?'

'Not really. I grabbed a sketchbook and some pencils from Mum's. I didn't get back to the vicarage to collect the rest of my stuff.'

'I expect we can get more pencils and sketchbooks and pastels or paints or whatever. You'll need to work on the table in the kitchen, though, for the messy stuff.'

How old did he think I was?

'And I'll give you some money so you can visit the castle and the priory ruins on your own whenever you like,' Dad continues. 'There are books in the bookshelves here too.'

This was worrying. Despite the fact that I was

supposed to only be here for the weekend, it sounded like Dad thought it might be a while before Mum got released.

'Is there Wi-Fi?' I asked, thinking of my phone.

'There is, but I don't know the code. I can get it from the owner. I deliberately didn't ask for it, so I could get on with work. There is Wi-Fi in the cafe, so when you get a hot chocolate you can use that, or maybe you can use mobile data?'

But what was the point? I suddenly realized I wasn't sure what I could even say to my friends. *Hi, everyone! Mum is in prison, just like Chloe said peace activists should be. By the way, can't meet up as I'm on an island off the coast of Northumbria.*

'So, anything else?' He seemed as keen as I was to finish the conversation. 'Maybe you'd like to go and explore a bit on your own – get your bearings?'

So he couldn't even bear to go for a walk with me. Fine. I'd go by myself.

I shrugged my shoulders.

'Turn right out of the door and go down to the main street. To the left is the road up to the castle. To the right are the shops, but I think they will have closed by now so the staff who live off the island can catch the tide. At least you'll see where they are.

You can take Stan if you like, though best to keep him on the lead.'

And you can get me out of the house. I understand.

But Stan could come. I loved him. Who couldn't love a mad red setter? I stuffed my sketchbook and a pencil in my coat pocket and called him. Stan bounded up to me, his tail wagging.

Grandad says Stan is one of life's enthusiasts. He just rushes at things, people, the world. It's funny that he is Dad's dog, because Dad doesn't rush at things. Neither do I. It's Mum who rushes at things. Stan should be her dog.

Anyway, Stan was the one thing – the one person – Dad and I could really talk about. Our only common ground.

Because it had got a bit hard talking to Dad.

I'm not sure why. I remember – or I think I remember – a time when it was easy. I loved my dad so much. All the photos of him and me when I was little – we look so happy together. He was young. I can see that now. He was only seventeen when I was born. That's younger than Eddie was when he went to Afghanistan, and I remember Nola telling me that her aunty Tina cried when he left and said he was too young. Mum cried too.

Maybe Dad was just too young to be my dad. Maybe if he had been older when he started, he'd have been better at talking to me now.

To think that Mum was even younger. Sixteen.

Just over two years older than me.

I couldn't imagine it.

Outside, the air was fresh and cleared my thoughts. Sparrows tweeted and chirped and fluttered in the hedge. I saw one further along the path stop, turn its head to look at us as Stan and I approached him, then hop away. We weren't even enough of a threat to make him bother to fly. A starling was across the road pecking the ground; its wings shining, two-tone. Up in the sky, I heard the cry of seagulls and saw them coasting in the air. Lucky things. No tide was stopping them going anywhere they wanted to.

Lindisfarne was beautiful, but my thoughts were like the tide, and once I was on my own I couldn't stop them rushing in. I couldn't stop thinking about the horrible things going on back at school. Why did life have to be so difficult?

I remember one of Grandad's friends saying that school days are the happiest days of your life. I don't know what school he went to.

I just wanted life to be simple. I just wanted to

have fun; to be back at home, planning with Nola and Chloe about what we'd do when we'd properly joined cadets. But first I would have to try to get Riya to talk to me again. And sort things out with Aidan.

I had to sort things out with Aidan.

Before it all got even more out of hand.

Chapter Four

We had an assembly just before we broke up for Easter, about our school setting up an army cadet training division this September. Isabel Hardy and Dan Peters from Year Ten were on the stage in army uniform, with a man called Major Lee. His face seemed familiar – maybe he had visited Grandad at some point. Anyway, Mrs Opie, our Head, introduced them and Major Lee explained that he had been talking to Mrs Opie about starting an army cadet group, only for students at our school. He said our PE teacher Miss Potter would be helping him as she was in the army reserves. I hadn't known that. Isabel and Dan talked about being in the town army cadets and they showed us a film about what they do and a bit about the summer camp they went on last year. It looked really good fun – lots of sport and camping and learning things you don't normally know; orienteering and first aid and stuff like that. And shooting. Marksmanship. Where else would I learn that? It's not exactly a normal school subject.

To be honest, I'd been wanting to be a cadet for ages. Obviously, being Grandad's granddaughter, this wasn't the first I had heard of them. Soon after I turned twelve, after we'd moved out, he mentioned it when I was back staying one weekend. He handed me a little book called *The Cadets' Handbook*.

'I thought you might be interested in this, Olivia. It gives the history of the cadets, its principles of fieldcraft, and map and compass work and first aid, signalling and so forth. The sort of thing they do. There is a detachment in the next town. I'm sure we could get you to meetings if you want to join.'

It was one of the few times I've seen Gran get really cross with him. She swivelled round from the oven top, where she was preparing our dinner.

'Andrew, what on earth are you doing? We should *not* be talking about this.'

'If Olivia wants to join the cadets, I think she should be allowed to,' said Grandad.

'I very much doubt if she has even thought about it. Have you, Olivia?'

I couldn't work out why Gran was getting so

worked up. She'd been an army wife for so many years – why would she be upset about me going to cadets?

'Not really,' I said. 'But I'd like to know more.'

'You see?' said Grandad.

'No,' said Gran. 'I'm sorry, Andrew, but I'm not going through this again. It has to come from the child.'

'But Olivia isn't like her father. She's far more sporty. She would love it, I'm sure,' said Grandad. He sounded rather pleading, which isn't like Grandad. But then it isn't like Gran to glare at him the way she did. She is so gentle and mild that when Gran glares it's a bit of a shock. Even for Grandad.

'Was Dad in the cadets, then? Didn't he like it? What happened?' I asked.

'I don't want to go into that, Olivia,' said Gran. 'You need to talk to your father about it. It was a long time ago and I don't really want to discuss it. But Andrew, I absolutely disagree with you bringing this up. Quite apart from anything else, Olivia is living with her mother now, and this will only cause trouble. I'm sorry, Olivia. If you want to go to army cadets, you will have to talk about it with your mother. If you really want to join and she agrees, we will do everything to support you – but we won't mention it again until we have the all-clear, is that understood?'

We both nodded. I remember that Gran sort of slammed the pie she had made down on to the table before slicing and serving it, and then we all very carefully talked about something else for the rest of dinner. Grandad didn't say anything more to me, and by the time of the assembly I still hadn't asked Mum about cadets. There hadn't seemed much point. It's run by the army, after all.

'Is Nola all right, seeing the uniforms and everything?' Riya whispered to me. 'You know, after Eddie . . .'

'Yeah, she's fine,' I whispered back. Because she was. Nola was next to me, looking up at the stage and smiling as they spoke, and you could see her eyes shining like it was Christmas. Everyone knew Eddie had been killed serving in the army. His funeral had been back in Year Seven, and now, in Year Nine, we didn't really talk much about him any more. I knew Nola had a picture of him in her room, and she said in RE once that sometimes she got very sad and went to the peace and remembrance garden in town to be quiet and think about him, but we didn't talk about him in our group of friends. I knew Eddie's death hadn't put her off the army, though. I think it made her more keen on it. Like her getting involved was honouring Eddie or something.

'This is amazing!' Nola said to us, on our way to PE. 'It's going to be so great having our own school detachment.'

I nodded, wondering what activities they'd let school cadets do, but I remember being distracted – we were going to use the climbing wall for the first time in PE, and I was quite excited about it. None of my group had ever done any climbing. Some people in the class had. I knew already that Aidan Brocklesby was really good at climbing. He's good at everything really, but he isn't irritating about it, unlike Seb Hughes. Seb walks down the corridor as if he thinks he is going to be mobbed by girls at any point, just because a small group of Year Seven and Eight girls think he is 'AMAZING' and giggle outside the practice room when his band plays. None of the Year Nine girls bother. We're tired of him. He is good-looking and he does sing well, but he knows it. And he's sort of boring. His favourite subject is himself.

Aidan is different. He's very clever and kind and

is interested in loads of things. I got to know him when we worked together on a science project in Year Seven. I remember at the beginning, Nola had a bit of a crush on him, and she and Riya would giggle and ask how I could concentrate around him and silly things like that. But even then I found he was easy to be with. We chose to do our project on birds. It turned out his mum and dad had taken him on birdwatching holidays to Scotland and other places – he already knew so much that I didn't feel silly telling him that I'd grown up doing loads of birdwatching with Grandad.

Our project ended up being really good and we both got an A. Aidan said he liked the way I drew birds. I was good at getting the colours right, and drawing them close up, but he was really good at the shapes they make when they fly. He drew a brilliant picture of a cormorant diving into the sea. The facts he knew about different birds were really interesting, too – he told me loads about birds in history, like how carrier pigeons were used to send messages in the World Wars, and some even got given medals!

Mum was so pleased about me getting an A. I remember her giving me a big hug when I got home. It was just me and her that evening. Back in

Year Seven, it was usually just her and me in the flat. I liked it then. She was often home when I got back. She was interested in me, and wanted to hear all about my day.

I remember Mum sitting at the kitchen table, bending her head to look at the folder. Aidan had said I could bring the folder back to show my mum and then take it to show my gran and grandad, and he would show his parents when I was finished.

'That's no problem,' he'd said, when I'd asked if he was sure. 'My little brother Finn might scribble on it anyway.'

I remember Mum pushing her hair back out of her eyes and saying, 'But these pictures are gorgeous, Olivia. You're both so good at drawing birds. What was the name of your partner, again?'

I hadn't told her in the first place, so the 'again' word was a bit of a trick question. I knew that as soon as I said a boy's name, she would get too casually not-bothered. Too I-think-it-is-fine-and-very-normal-for-girls-and-boys-to-be-friends-and-it-makes-me-cross-how-the-media-make-such-a-big-deal-of-it-and-I'm-certainly-not-getting-overexcited-and-why-don't-you-bring-him-back-to-tea? sort of casual.

'Aidan,' I said. 'Aidan Brocklesby.'

She looked up. 'Brocklesby? He must be Phil and Elizabeth's son. I met them at a talk about peacemaking recently.'

She was really pleased. And more pleased about the fact he was the *Brocklesbys'* son than the Brocklesbys' *son*, if you see what I mean. Which was a relief.

Funny thing was that Grandad and Gran had the same reaction.

'The Brocklesby lad?' said Grandad. 'They are a lovely family. Phil Brocklesby's an excellent GP. Very good man. Has a real heart for the underprivileged.'

'Oh yes, and I meet Elizabeth at the food bank,' said Gran. 'She brings her little boy with her to help. She's a lovely woman.'

Anyway, it was really nice doing that Year Seven project with Aidan, and after that I saw him quite a lot really. I saw him with his dad at a few of the birdwatching Saturdays I went on with Grandad, and I met him and his mum when I went to help Gran weed the peace and remembrance garden in the town. It's a beautiful place, the garden. It was a wasteland, and then people decided to clear it and make it a place for people to go and sit. One of the benches there has Eddie's name on it. It's the one Nola sometimes sits on when she is sad about him.

I remember once when Aidan was helping out with Finn. Finn was really sweet, toddling round with his bucket and spade, and kept giving me weeds as presents.

'No, Finn. Olivia doesn't want that,' said Aidan, taking yet another dandelion from him. 'She is trying to get rid of the weeds, she doesn't want more.'

Finn flung himself down on the ground as if the worst thing in the world had happened, and started to sob.

'I don't mind, really,' I said to Aidan, taking the dandelion from his little brother. I knelt down next to Finn. 'Finn, don't cry. Thank you *so* much. It's a beautiful flower.'

Finn kept crying, but you could tell that he was listening to himself now and quite enjoying the drama. Then he opened one eye and saw me holding the dandelion and immediately cheered up.

'Get fuffy for Livvy,' he said, and went off, tear-stained and snotty and very determined to get another one from the pile of weeding next to his mum.

'Thanks,' said Aidan. 'He really likes you.'

'I really like him,' I said. 'I'd like to have a little brother.'

Aidan's mum said something to Gran and they both beamed at me.

'Thanks, love,' called his mum. 'That's very kind.'

And then, in the summer after Year Seven ended, Mum and I went camping, to a wood owned by Johnny's friends. They invite people to come and join them and do things like art and building shelters, or sitting round the fires, or just relaxing. And when we got there, Aidan and his mum and dad and Finn were already there. It turned out they were friends of Johnny's friends too.

So for a week then, and again last summer before the start of Year Nine, I went on holiday with Aidan. There were about five other families, and there were other older children there too, so we all sort of formed a gang. There was a zip wire, and trees to climb, and loads of things to do – like even driving a kind of tractor with a trailer. We built a huge pizza oven out of sand and clay and bricks, and celebrated by making a pizza at the end of the week. At night, we sat around the fire and told ghost stories or played wink murder, or Johnny and Phil – Aidan's dad – got their guitars out and we sang songs. And we played with Finn. Aidan and I played loads with Finn – we read him stories, cuddled him and tickled him. Mum got on really well with Elizabeth, Aidan's mum, so we spent a lot of time outside their tent and sitting with them at meals.

So, what I'm trying to say is, I already knew loads about Aidan outside of school. I knew how funny he was, and how he was really good at telling lies in games and climbing very high. I knew he could do impressions, and used too much washing-up liquid and then had an annoying habit of flicking bubbles at me. I knew he took making pizzas far too seriously but laughed at his own awful jokes, and I knew he was really kind to Finn.

But in between those times, when we were at school, we didn't really speak. It wasn't that we weren't friends any more, it was just like we had pressed a pause button. Family camping holidays or seeing each other at weekends when we were birdwatching were a different world. We didn't need to explain this to each other. We just knew.

It has never been easy for girls and boys to just be friends in our school. Some people in Year Nine went out with each other and sometimes I could imagine liking Aidan that way, but I didn't really want to make my life more complicated. It was bad enough already, moving out of Mum's and back to Gran and Grandad's. I didn't want any more drama. I've never enjoyed it. I'd seen enough arguments between Grandad and Mum, in Year Six. It was nice when things were peaceful.

I wished they still were.

Chapter Five

Anyway, after the special assembly it was PE, and we got to the climbing wall and partnered up. Nola and Riya went together, and I thought Chloe and I would go together, but Miss Potter put Chloe with Seb. Nola and Riya and I have been friends with Chloe since she came in Year Nine, but she didn't mind being with Seb. Their families know each other, like mine knows the Brocklesbys.

'I've got a feeling you're going to take to this, Olivia,' Miss Potter said. 'I'm teaming you up with Aidan, who is already very experienced on a climbing wall.'

'I'll belay,' said Aidan, 'and you can climb.'

'What's belaying?' I said.

'There's a rope attached to the top of the climbing wall, and it is going to be attached to you but also to me, so that if you fall you'll still be safe — I can pull on the rope to make sure you don't hit the ground, though there is a mat here.'

We both wore harnesses and helmets and he stood at the bottom of the wall and held the rope as I climbed.

'Look down to figure out the next place for your feet, rather than up for the next hand holds,' he advised me, 'and take it steady.'

It was fun. I was a bit nervous at first, but I liked planning where to go. I got about two-thirds up without too much bother.

'You're doing really well,' he said.

I felt proud. I knew the main reason I was able to concentrate on doing well was that I felt completely safe with Aidan. I could trust him to look after me – he was concentrating on me all the time, and I knew that he knew what he was doing and would never let me fall.

Miss Potter came to check on us.

'Excellent, Olivia. You're a natural, I can see. And that's ideal tension on the ropes, Aidan. Good teamwork. Now, Olivia, Aidan will belay you down, and I can teach you how to belay him.'

Going down was even more scary than going up, as you were more aware of how far you had to fall.

But, again, I listened to Aidan more than the fear, and it went well. Then we swapped roles.

Miss Potter took teaching me about belaying very seriously. I liked that. It made it feel important and exciting. She stayed with me and checked I was belaying properly as Aidan climbed quickly to the very top of the wall and then back down again. He was brilliant. As usual.

'Is this the sort of thing we would do in cadets?' I asked.

'Yes. Oh good, does that mean you are thinking of joining, then?' she replied.

'Yes. My grandad is a major in the reserves,' I said. 'He's an army chaplain. He went to Afghanistan.' I found I wanted to impress her.

'That's great!' said Miss Potter. 'Does he live near here? Would I know him? Is his name Wilding too?'

'No. He's a vicar – Andrew Harvey,' I said.

'Oh! I know who he is!' Miss Potter beamed. 'I had no idea you were related to Major Harvey. He's marvellous. You must be so proud.'

'I am,' I said.

'Well, cadets will be right up your street, then,' said Miss Potter. 'How about you, Aidan?'

'I don't think so,' said Aidan, undoing his harness.

'That's a shame,' said Miss Potter, sounding surprised. 'May I ask why?'

'It would be a bit difficult, because my family are Quakers,' said Aidan.

'Oh, I see,' said Miss Potter. 'That's a shame,' she repeated. 'I mean, from our point of view, of course, not that I don't respect your family's ideals.' She looked flustered, which wasn't like her at all. It was a bit awkward, and suddenly Miss Potter was calling us together and Aidan had gone to stand with Abhishek and Gareth, and I was standing with Nola and Riya. Seb and Chloe were still standing together and laughing, but they saw Nola nudging me to look at them and Chloe came over straight away.

'What?' she said to Nola.

'Nothing!' said Nola, rolling her eyes.

'You did so well, Olivia,' said Chloe. 'I heard Miss Potter talking to you about cadets. Are you going to join?'

'Yes, probably,' I said. I didn't want to think about the letter they'd given out at the end of assembly – with the permission slip for a parent to sign. It wasn't Mum's business anyway. I mean, it would be in school, at lunchtimes. Why did she even have to know? I didn't tell her about what I was doing in physics, like, 'Mum, I'm learning about gravity, is that OK?'

'Aidan would be fantastic in cadets,' said Nola.

'I don't think he is going to join,' I said.

'How come?' said Chloe.

'Why not?' asked Nola.

'His family are Quakers.'

'What's that got to do with it?' said Nola. 'I mean, it doesn't matter if your family are born somewhere else. Like, there are the Gurkhas. They are really important in the British army, and they're from Nepal.'

'Where do Quakers come from, then?' said Chloe. 'I thought Aidan's parents were Irish.'

'It's not about coming from somewhere. Quakers are a type of Christian,' I explained.

'Oh, I know!' said Nola. 'They had something to do with the peace and remembrance garden. Aunty said the Quakers gave some money to help it. They provided Eddie's bench.'

'I think Quakers have something to do with pacifism,' said Riya. 'I think they don't agree with wars. So I'm pretty sure they don't join the army cadets.'

I knew she was right, but I didn't really want

to get involved in talking about it. I had more than enough politics to deal with at home, and I'd largely managed to keep my home stuff out of school, so far.

'I think we should talk to him about it,' said Nola. 'I mean, nobody likes wars. He can be a Quaker, but he shouldn't think he isn't welcome in cadets. You can ask him, Olivia. You've been his partner.'

'Let's just leave it,' I said. 'Miss Potter has already tried.'

'Well, I'll do it then,' said Nola. 'We'll need him in cadets. He can help the rest of us get better at climbing. I'm going to tell him so.'

Chapter Six

Dad was right. The shops were all closed, except for the village store, but I couldn't go in there with a dog. Stan decided to do a poo in the street, so I cleared it up and tracked down a red and black dog waste bin. There was one just round the corner from our house, before the path leading up to the castle, near the beach.

I liked seeing the sea and smelling the salt in the air. If it hadn't been for all the stuff about Mum and Aidan and Riya going round and round my head, I could see that I might even have liked being there.

It's not exactly cheering knowing your mum is in a police cell, your dad doesn't want you around, and your friendships are a mess.

Stan pulled me away from the road and across to the beach, his feathery tail waving joyfully.

There is a boy about my age sitting alone on some rocks, sketching. For a moment I think it is Aidan, and my heart starts to hammer. I nearly turn to go the other way, until I realize that of course it isn't Aidan at all, just someone who looks a bit like him. The boy who is not Aidan is wearing some sort of long overcoat and, even at a distance, I can see that, like Aidan, he is really good at art.

Stan seems to like him too, and pulls so hard I let go of the lead. He hurtles his way towards the boy and jumps up on him, making him drop his sketchbook.

'Sorry!' I shout.

'Hello, boy!' the boy says to Stan, making a fuss of him so that Stan is in heaven. I grab Stan and pull him back.

'I'm so sorry,' I say, my hand on Stan's collar.

The boy, who is still stroking Stan, jumps when I speak, as if he hadn't noticed me yelling and charging towards them. He is tall and thin, the same sort of build as Aidan, but he has fair hair.

'I hope your work isn't spoilt,' I say, struggling to stop Stan jumping up at him.

'Um . . . no. Thank you. Who are you?' he says.

'I'm Olivia,' I say.

'I'm William. Pleased to meet you,' he says. He sounds posh. Posh but nice. He has a voice like Johnny, and Mum said Johnny went to public school. He puts out his hand for me to shake, which takes me by surprise. I can't imagine shaking hands with Aidan or Gareth or Abhishek. I keep hold of Stan's collar with my left hand and awkwardly put my right hand out. When I go to Grandad's church, everybody shakes hands at the bit where Grandad asks us to give each other the sign of peace, and sometimes people grip your hand too tight, or their hands are limp or hot and sweaty. This boy William's handshake is just right. He's a bit odd, but somehow I like him straight away.

'So, is this is your dog?'

'Well, my dad's dog really,' I say. 'His name is Stan.'

We both stroke him. I can't think of anything to say, and the boy doesn't speak either, but it doesn't feel strange. It is a friendly silence.

'I'd better go,' he says. He picks up his sketchbook and puts it in a leather satchel. 'I'm a guest up at the castle, so I'd better not be late.'

'Oh, I didn't know people could stay at the castle,' I say.

'It's quite a new thing, I believe. My father's friend designed the accommodation, and he often stays there himself with his family. I don't really know them, but they said I could come and stay and get some sea air, after being ill.'

'Oh, I'm sorry you were ill,' I say, a bit awkwardly.

'Thank you. I'm feeling much better now. Well . . . Olivia . . . it was nice to meet you.'

He is so polite. Quite formal. I like it. The boys in our class could be a bit politer. Not Aidan, to be fair – even when he was angry with me, he was polite.

William shakes my hand again, then hoists his leather bag over his shoulder and sets back up the road to the castle.

Stan woofed, nudging my hand. I attached his lead and we walked back. I sneaked a look over to the castle path, but the boy wasn't there. I guessed he had probably decided to walk back around by the shore.

Stan pulled on the lead the whole way home. He seemed to know the way. I'd forgotten Dad and he had been living there a few weeks now. He was as eager to see Dad again as if they had been separated for years.

'Did you have a good time, then?' Dad said, making a fuss of Stan.

'Yes, OK,' I said, but I wasn't sure if he was talking to the dog or to me.

Dinner smelt delicious. Dad was making a pasta bake with salmon and cream, and garlic bread. He's an amazing cook. Gran told me that Dad started learning to cook as soon as he knew he was going to be my dad. Apparently he bought a cookery book, learnt the recipes and insisted on cooking one for Mum and Gran and Grandad every night. It was his way of coping.

Gran told me that out of the blue one day when I was visiting. I didn't really know what to say. I wasn't cross Dad hadn't married Mum when I was born, or anything else Gran was apparently worrying about. Gran had come up to the room in the vicarage, where I was trying to paint a still life. She'd brought me a cup of tea, but really she just wanted an excuse to talk.

'You know your dad really loves you, don't you? You know he wanted to marry your mum and look after you both,' she said, looking a bit anxious. 'We had a real struggle persuading him to stay in school. He was always such a kind, serious boy. He was so in love with your mum. He wanted to marry her and go out and get a job and find somewhere to live with her. But she didn't want to marry him. She was determined not to, because she said she was too young to make a commitment to him for life, and having a baby was the wrong reason to get married. And you know your mum – when she is determined not to do something, nothing can make her do it.

'So we told him not to worry. We told him we'd look after her – and you – and she could come and live with us, because she was living in a hostel at the time. He was only seventeen. He was better off finishing his A levels. He had his offer from Durham to study history – everybody said he would do so well. He did do so well. We're so proud of him, with his doctorate and lecturing job. But he didn't want to leave you – you know that, Olivia?'

'I know, Gran. I don't mind,' I said, taking the mug of tea. 'Honestly, loads of people don't live with their parents. It isn't a problem. Other people live with aunts or uncles or foster parents, and nobody minds. Nola and Eddie lived with their aunt and uncle all through primary school before Eddie died and Nola's still there. Riya lives with her mum and dad and her brothers and her gran and grandad. I don't need to live with my parents. I don't *want* to live with my parents. Either of them. I want to live with you.'

'I know. I just don't think you see enough of your dad. He doesn't look so happy these days. It's good he has that job in Durham, but it's so far away. I wish he could find someone. He never seemed to get over your mum. He has done so well with his studies and his career. But you're all he's got as family. Well, you and your grandad and me.'

'And Stan – don't forget Stan,' I said.

Gran laughed a little, but her face was still a bit anxious. 'You're everything to him, Olivia. Try to talk to him a little more. He's shy. It's hard for him, not living near you. And you don't seem to chat to him the way you used to. If you don't talk to him, he won't talk back. He was never very good at small talk.'

I knew what Gran meant, but it didn't really make things easier.

I saw Dad and Stan every month, when he came down to Gran and Grandad's for the weekend. We used to do lots of things together – go to London for the museums and galleries and to look at the dinosaurs in Crystal Palace Park . . . When I was younger I really liked his visits. I looked forward to them. Dad was my hero. But then Dad went away for three months to America when I started Year Eight – Gran and Grandad looked after Stan – and something had changed by the time Dad came back. I suppose I'd changed. I felt like I didn't know what to say to him any more. I didn't really want to spend the day going to museums and galleries – I had too much homework. I ended up just seeing Dad for Sunday dinner over at Gran and Grandad's, so we didn't really spend much time together on our own. The only thing we did together was walk Stan.

And so there we were, sitting down to dinner, on our own, with plenty of time to talk to each other. But I couldn't really start from scratch and tell him all about my life.

There wasn't much to say.

Or, perhaps, there was too much.

Chapter Seven

'So, school. Is it going OK?' said Dad, as he put the pasta on my plate.

That was a pretty big question. Did he mean, 'How do you think school is going academically?' If so, pretty well. I always got my work done on time. My marks were fine. More than fine, really. I was like him – booky. But I was quite sporty too, and that was a bit more like Grandad.

But we both knew he didn't just mean school. We both knew he really meant, 'How do you think life is going AS A WHOLE?'

And there were two answers to that.

A and B.

Answer A: Part One
Well, Dad, I could have said, it's all gone a bit wrong, actually.

Not at first. Year Nine was going well, especially when we went back after Easter. Miss Potter teamed me and Aidan up a lot on the climbing wall, and then Mr Amis, our form teacher, teamed us up in art as well.

'Ask Aidan about joining the cadets,' hissed Nola at me, when we were collecting materials to draw each other's portraits. 'I haven't had a chance.'

'I can't,' I said back quickly. 'I don't even talk to him. Not really. Just leave it, Nola.'

The good thing about being teamed up in art is that you don't need to chat. Once I got over feeling a bit shy at doing it, Mr Amis was so technical about teaching us to look at each other that I could just concentrate on getting Aidan's nose and mouth and eyes right. I liked Aidan's face, the shape of it. I liked his eyebrows.

I liked the way Aidan drew me too – he really looked at me, trying to be accurate. It is difficult drawing someone else – getting the proportions right, the perspective. We had to keep changing what we had done.

'Hey, my nose is a bit big!' said Aidan, once.

'What about my chin?' I said.

But, basically, we both wanted to get it right.

Mr Amis was very pleased.

'These are two excellent portraits,' he said. 'You've properly looked at each other.' He put them on the wall.

That's the sort of thing I used to run home to the vicarage to tell everyone about, when I was at primary school. I'd rush in and find Mum and Gran and Grandad, to announce that my pictures were up on the classroom wall. Did they ever tell you, Dad?

Anyway, Chloe nudged me when Mr Amis said Aidan and I had properly looked at each other, which was a bit embarrassing, but she's like the rest of her family – really open and friendly – so I didn't mind. I've been to her house a few times. Chloe's got a sweet little brother and sister, and her dad is smiley and good at jokes and magic tricks – you'd really like this card trick he showed me, Dad – and her mum is ever so kind to animals and keeps rescuing ill ones. The Sinclairs are lovely, but their newspaper is the one Mum hates, and they are very worried about 'scroungers' and people from other countries coming here and 'swamping' our country. Mum says the newspapers exaggerate things to make people scared, but I couldn't exactly say that when they were talking about it over dinner.

It was a bit difficult sometimes, when they said things about refugees not really needing help, or just being terrorists in disguise; things that I disagreed with, but they were so chatty and noisy that I don't think they ever noticed I was quiet at those bits of the conversation. And they were very kind to me – they kept telling me how glad they were I was friends with Chloe, and how grateful they were to me and the others for making her welcome.

I never invited Chloe back to the flat, of course. I couldn't imagine what she would think of Mum, and I didn't want Mum to ask her things either. You know what Mum's like – she's got this habit of ranting on about things she cares about, and taking it for granted everyone agrees with her. Chloe came to the vicarage at weekends sometimes, and Gran was always pleased when I brought my friends to meet her, so it worked out well. Gran is very good at small talk. Not like Mum. Chloe's parents loved Gran, when they came to pick her up, and Chloe's dad was impressed that Grandad's in the army and has met the queen and everything. Chloe's dad is really into 'being British' and stuff like that, like Grandad.

It would have been a disaster if they had come to our flat. I know they would have said something about the anti-war posters in the kitchen and loo, or they would have talked about politics, and Mum would never have just agreed with them or kept quiet. I mean, after all, Mum and Grandad had so many rows about war that we ended up moving out of the vicarage and into the flat above Johnny's in town.

No, Dad, in case you ask – no, I don't bring anyone home to Mum's flat. Not after Year Six and the poppies. Not after Emily Reed and her friends stopped inviting me to their parties, as a result. I decided that for secondary school it was safer if nobody knew about my home life or my mum's opinions. I knew Nola and Riya from primary school, but I'm sure they've never told anyone. They know I don't want any fuss.

It's OK in my group of friends, because Riya doesn't really bring people home either and Nola comes over to the vicarage to see me when I stay there. I did try bringing her back to the flat, once, but that's never going to happen again. At least that wasn't because of Mum. Nola and her uncle and aunt have known Mum for ages. Mum came to Eddie's funeral and cried. They don't agree with her views, but they love each other. No, it was more because of Mum's new friends. You can never be quite sure who will be there, these days. Most of them, like Sister Mary, are gentle and kind – but there are a couple who get really angry about things and go on and on. Johnny says it's surprising how cross some pacifists can get. Anyway, Nola got really upset because she came back to the flat and a not very gentle friend of Johnny's was there, and he was swearing about the army. Mum told him to be quiet and gave Nola a hug, but after that, I didn't want Nola to risk bumping into him again. The vicarage is just safer.

The funny thing is that the only other person from school who has ever been back to our flat is Aidan, when Johnny and Mum had a meeting, the Saturday after Easter. I remember opening the front door and being surprised to see Aidan with his mum and little brother, sitting on our sofa.

I nearly stayed in, but I'd already organized to go out with Nola and Chloe.

That must have been when it was all arranged.

I don't know if you know, Dad, but there was another demonstration before the one Mum got arrested for – two weeks into the summer term. It was outside our local army base. Mum was interviewed on the local news about why she and fifty other demonstrators had lain down in the road to symbolize civilians killed by drone warfare. Mum had told me what they were going to do, and she had invited me to come, but I'd said I didn't really want to. She didn't put any pressure on me or anything. That isn't Mum's style.

I do know that.

And it isn't that I think it is good that civilians are killed by drones. It's just that I wasn't sure if lying in the road was going to help. And, basically, I was just too embarrassed.

Anyway, I knew they were going to do it, but, stupidly, I didn't realize they were going to be on the news.

Mum was going away with Johnny somewhere after the demonstration – some conference on peace, I think – so I was staying back at the vicarage while they were away, and Gran was making a big fuss of me. We were about to have lunch, when Grandad got a phone call.

'Do you mind if I put the TV on?' he said to Gran after hanging up. 'The base said there is something on the local news that I should see.'

'We can take our lunch in on trays,' said Gran.

'It's nice to live on the wild side now and then!'

Gran can have fun doing anything.

Grandad switched on the TV and a familiar face filled the screen.

'Oh no! It's Mum!' I said.

'What on earth . . .?' said Grandad.

'What's happening?' said Gran.

Mum only spoke for a few moments, but she got straight to the point.

'My companions are lying in the road to bring home to the government and the British public the obscene amount of civilian deaths in wartime. War is not a video game. Most people who die in modern wars are not soldiers but civilians, and more children are killed than soldiers every year. We have to acknowledge this.'

There was an interview with a very cross lorry driver, who'd had to take a different route through town. A police officer said that it was regrettable that there had been disruption, but the situation had been resolved peacefully.

Grandad snorted. 'Of course there was disruption. What on earth do they think they were doing? It is so irresponsible.'

'Oh, I'm so dead,' I muttered.

'What do you mean, Olivia?' Gran said, sounding really worried.

'It doesn't matter,' I said.

'Yes, it does,' said Grandad.

'It's just . . . It's just that, apart from Nola and Riya, nobody at secondary school knows Mum is a pacifist and does things like this,' I said. 'Not even Chloe. Her mum and dad would go mad. And at school, nobody cares about pacifism or politics or things like that. We're going to have army cadets and everyone's really excited.'

'Oh yes,' Grandad said. He looked over at Gran. 'Are you interested?'

'Andrew,' said Gran, warningly. 'I do think Caz should be the one having this conversation.'

'I'm Olivia's grandfather, Ruth,' said Grandad. 'Why can't I talk to my own granddaughter about this? And it is completely different this time – this is about something which is happening at her school, after all. We're not talking about a detachment in another town.'

'I'd like to do it, yes,' I said. 'But I don't think Mum will exactly be keen.'

'Well, we'll see about that,' said Grandad.

'Andrew, leave it. And don't worry about what

your friends will make of this, Olivia,' Gran said, nodding at the telly. 'I'm sure it will all be fine. Nobody will remember it.'

It was awful, Dad. That Sunday, I went to bed with a feeling of doom, and it stayed with me as I caught the bus from outside the vicarage to school the next day. Nobody said anything to me at the lockers, and I began to hope that nobody had seen the news or guessed it was my mum. I thought I'd got away with not having to worry about it.

But then I was walking along the corridor towards my form room for registration, and I saw Mr Amis and Nola coming along the corridor from the opposite direction. We all reached the form room together just in time to hear Chloe saying loudly, 'My dad had big problems with his deliveries because of them. He thinks they should be locked up and the key should be thrown away. He says they're terrorist sympathizers. They're threatening national security, when our country is already under threat by terrorism. He says, in the old days, they'd be shot as traitors.'

I had a horrible feeling in my stomach.

'Sounds a bit extreme, Chloe,' said Mr Amis, as we entered the class. 'Who would have been shot?'

'Those peace activists outside the army base at the weekend,' she said. 'Whose side are they on, anyway?'

I took my seat next to Nola and whispered, 'It was Mum. She was on the news.'

'I know,' she whispered back. 'But Chloe doesn't.'

'I'm going to have to tell her, I suppose,' I said. 'Better it comes from me.'

But before I could do anything, Aidan had put up his hand.

'I was one of them,' he said.

Chapter Eight

Answer A: Part Two

I'm telling you, Dad, I don't know how Aidan was so brave. There was a sort of gasp from the rest of the class. Chloe went red with embarrassment. I don't think she realised she'd actually know one of the people her dad wanted shot. I don't think her dad realized she knew any of them either, to be honest.

Seb booed.

'Be quiet, everyone,' said Mr Amis firmly. 'And, Seb, that is totally out of order. We should be able to talk about local and national politics without being offensive to one another. We have form time now, and this is interesting local news. Aidan, do you want to explain why you were at the demonstration?'

He nodded. 'Well, I'm a Quaker . . .' he said.

'Wait a minute, Aidan,' said Mr Amis. 'Is everyone clear about who Quakers are?'

Riya put up her hand. 'They're some sort of Christians? And they are pacifists, so they don't agree with fighting in wars?' she said.

'Excellent,' said Mr Amis. 'So, Aidan, were there only Quakers at this demo, then?'

'No, it wasn't only Quakers,' said Aidan.

I kept my head down, so I couldn't see if he was looking at me. I knew I could have said something about Mum, but I really didn't want to get into it. I mean, at least Aidan agreed with his parents. It wasn't fair if I had to explain about pacifism when I didn't agree with it. What Mum felt and thought about things dominated too much of my life. Even when she wasn't with me, I was thinking about things she was thinking about, or thinking about not thinking about them. I just wanted a break from her world for a bit. Time just to think my own thoughts, and come to my own conclusions without her voice inside my head, arguing with me about it.

'And we were there because we wanted to remind everyone that ordinary people get killed in wars,' Aidan said, 'and make people think about that.'

Seb put up his hand.

'Yes?' said Mr Amis.

'Please, sir. Everyone knows people get killed

in wars. We don't need people lying in the road to show us.'

Riya put up her hand too.

'Yes, Riya?' said Mr Amis. You could see he was relieved she had put up her hand, as she was bound to be more polite than Seb.

'It's true. How can we forget about wars? We hear about them all the time. Like on television and in the newspapers.'

I liked the way Riya asked her question. It wasn't like she was asking it because she thought Aidan was stupid, the way Seb did. She didn't understand exactly why Aidan had done the demonstration, but she really wanted to.

I glanced over at Nola. I was a bit worried that she would start thinking about Eddie and get upset.

'Aidan, I have to agree with these points,' said Mr Amis. 'Can you explain to us why your demo would make us think about war more than all the images we already see? If seeing injured children doesn't put us off war, then why would what you did work?'

'I think it was really stupid,' said Seb.

'And I think that if you can't contribute more intelligently to this conversation, Seb, you should leave. One more interruption and you are out,' said

Mr Amis. He was really cross, and he isn't one of those teachers who gets cross very much. Seb folded his arms and looked sulky.

'I know it caused a few problems, but if it hadn't, nobody would have paid attention. I think it is like poppies,' said Aidan. 'You can use something to symbolize something else. You wear a flower, and somehow it makes you think of people being killed. Except maybe we are too used to the image of poppies now, and don't really think about what they mean any more. So instead of a poppy to stand for a dead body in war, you have live bodies laying down, to shock people and remind them that the dead bodies were once alive. I don't know how to explain it, really. It's like art making you look at something in a different way. And getting people to talk about stuff and not take things for granted. Like wars.'

'But we have to have wars,' said Chloe. 'I mean, if someone is attacking you, you have to defend yourself.'

'Maybe we don't have to have wars,' said Aidan. 'Maybe we should look more at what causes them and try to solve arguments earlier. Not wait until it gets so bad that we are attacking each other.'

'Well, anyway,' said Chloe, 'my dad says that

demonstrations waste police time and we need the police to fight terrorists.'

'You could argue,' said Mr Amis, 'that one of the important things we are defending against terrorism is our right to free speech. So if we stop pacifists expressing their beliefs, we are supporting terrorist ideals.'

'So, are you one of them, sir?' said Gareth. 'A pacifist?'

'I don't have to answer that,' said Mr Amis. 'It's not a teacher's job to tell you what to think or to tread a political party line – it's my job to give you the tools to let you work things out for yourselves and make your own decisions. This has been a very interesting discussion. Thank you, Aidan. I have to say that if the demonstration was done to make people talk about the issues of war, then it certainly seems to have succeeded.'

We had PE straight after form time, and we all headed down to the hall. Aidan was walking with Abhishek and Gareth, and I noticed Seb and Josh run past them and give Aidan a push, so that he lost his balance and fell into Abhishek.

'Hey, what do you think you're doing?' said Gareth to Seb.

'I don't like terrorist sympathizers,' said Seb, and then I saw him looking back at Chloe, who was walking next to me.

'What an idiot,' said Riya.

Aidan didn't respond or push him or say anything. He just ignored him and kept on walking.

'Who are you calling a terrorist?' said Abhishek, turning back.

Seb put up his hands. 'Look, mate, nothing personal. Unless you've got something to tell me? I mean, those are clearly the sort of people Aidan likes to hang out with . . .'

'Hey!' said Riya. 'I'm telling Mrs Opie.'

Seb and his friends just ran ahead, laughing.

'I'm going to Mrs Opie at breaktime,' said Riya. 'That's so racist.' She looked really worried.

'I'll come with you,' Gareth said. 'I don't know why they involved Abhishek like that, or pushed Aidan in the first place.'

'I didn't do anything,' said Abhishek, shaking his head as if he couldn't believe it had happened.

Riya looked at me and I was about to say I'd go with them, but I hesitated, and then Chloe got involved.

'Well, it's really Aidan Brocklesby's fault,' she said.

'Seb isn't a racist. He was talking about Aidan, not Abhishek. Nothing would have happened if he hadn't started it.'

'What did Aidan do wrong?' said Riya. 'Seb didn't need to push him like that.'

'Aidan doesn't care that he made things difficult for people in town or that he wasted police time doing stupid demonstrations outside our army base,' said Chloe. 'Haven't we got enough problems keeping this country safe? Surely you don't agree with him?'

'So what if I do?' said Riya. 'Even if I don't, it's like Mr Amis says – Aidan has a right to be a pacifist, and only a stupid person would think he hasn't.'

'Who are you calling stupid?' said Chloe. 'Are you saying my dad is stupid?'

'Maybe I am,' said Riya, glaring at her.

I couldn't believe it. Riya was so quiet and polite normally. I was glad to get to PE. They couldn't keep arguing in the lesson. It was so awkward. I was beginning to think that sooner or later I would have to say something, get involved – and I didn't know how. How could I support either of my friends, when I could kind of see where they were both coming from? My best friends were arguing. I'd never seen Riya or Chloe that angry before. Well, I had actually, at the beginning of Year Nine when they both noticed some Year Eights being mean to a kitten, just outside the school. Riya and Chloe had both run across the road and shouted at them, and Nola and I ran after them to see what was happening. Chloe had taken the kitten home to her family, and that was how we had all got to be friends. Now they were really angry at each other. And that wasn't good.

But I didn't know what I could do, Dad. I didn't want to get dragged into this whole pacifist stuff. I didn't want people to take sides. It seemed like I couldn't even escape politics at school now, and it just made me feel fed up.

We went into the hall and Chloe walked straight over to Seb, ready for the lesson. Gareth and Abhishek were partners. Riya and Nola stood next to them, and I went over to Aidan as usual.

It wasn't a very good session. I kept thinking about the row and the fact that no one knew my mum had been at the demonstration they were all so angry about, with Aidan. I might not agree with her, but I didn't want to hear them say things about her — the way they were talking about Aidan. I knew Mum didn't support terrorism. I knew she was only trying to do the right thing. But I still felt annoyed with her. She made my life so complicated, just by being her.

I found it very hard to concentrate, and made some stupid mistakes climbing. Normally Aidan was really kind and encouraging, but this time he hardly said anything. I felt he was cross with me and I could sort of guess why. He must have been expecting me to support him during form time, but how could I tell him that just because he's seen me with my mum and her friends, it doesn't mean I agree with it all totally? I'm not a pacifist. I've got a right not to be a pacifist. But then, I didn't exactly support him in the corridor either, and that was just plain bullying . . . And that makes me a coward.

'Everything OK?' said Miss Potter, coming over to us. I sort of nodded, without looking at Aidan. He must have done the same, as Miss Potter continued, 'Olivia, I hear that your grandad has offered to come to talk to the school next week, about his time in Afghanistan as an army chaplain.'

'I didn't know that,' I said.

'Yes. We're really pleased. And he's agreed to help advise the school on setting up our army cadet division.'

'Yay!' said Nola, who had overheard.

'That's brilliant of Olivia's grandad!' said Chloe.

I could feel Riya looking at me, but I didn't quite want to meet her eyes. I had a feeling she thought I should say something and share my opinions about this stupid argument or my mum being a pacifist, because my grandad was helping set up the cadets. But I didn't only have one opinion, so I couldn't say anything. I didn't particularly want Aidan to know how much I really wanted to join the cadets and how much I didn't agree with Mum. They weren't anything to do with us climbing together or drawing each other. I didn't want things to change. Why couldn't we keep different parts of our lives separate, and carry on as we always did, like normal?

But I found I couldn't look at Aidan. And that wasn't normal at all.

Seb and Chloe were doing really well together, which was a bit annoying, and Miss Potter asked them to demonstrate belaying each other and climbing up the first third of the wall, which I think went to Seb's head.

'Miss, am I better than Aidan?' said Seb. 'Is he quaking in his boots, because I am so good?'

Josh laughed, which was normal, but so did Julia Brown and Maria Duffy, which was not very nice.

And, worst of all, so did Chloe. Nobody normally laughed at Aidan like that. I didn't like it.

Miss Potter didn't like it either. She is never usually cross, but she looked really fed up and grumpy. She glared at Seb.

'Hardly,' she said. 'Believe me, Seb, you have a long way to go before you're as good as Aidan Brocklesby.'

You could see Seb didn't like that at all. He stopped smirking and looked sulky.

'Aidan, perhaps you would like to demonstrate?' She gave Aidan an encouraging smile and he nodded.

'I'll belay you,' said Miss Potter. 'Now, Seb, watch and learn. And maybe you'll be a little less quick to make a fool of yourself in future.'

Aidan was amazing, Dad. You could see him looking at the wall, planning the route and assessing the risks. I saw him stretching for holds I thought he couldn't reach and bridging gaps I thought were impossible – but he was steady and sure, and his feet and hands found each point he went for. He didn't seem to be rushing, but he was at the top of the wall so quickly. And then he was down it again super fast, and people were clapping. He smiled and gave a mock bow. He looked a lot happier.

The lesson ended so well, but then Nola rushed over when we were leaving the hall, and messed everything up.

'You were fantastic!' she said. 'You've got to join the cadets, Aidan. I'm sure it doesn't matter to them that you're a Quaker.'

'It does matter to me, Nola,' he said, and sighed and walked off.

'That was a bit rude,' said Nola, hurt.

'What's that?' said Seb, walking over and poking his nose in. He was smiling, turning on all his charm. 'What's the matter, Quaker Boy?' he shouted after Aidan, sort of half laughing. 'Scared of cadets, then?'

But Aidan had turned the corner already. I didn't think he had heard, and I didn't want any more rows, so I didn't say anything. Maybe I should have.

'So, Olivia, I hear your grandad is a major in the army?' said Seb, walking along the corridor with me, Chloe and Nola.

I think it was actually the first time Seb had ever bothered to talk to me. He wasn't sulky or cross like in class – he was really smiley – and I couldn't help it, there was a bit of me that liked that he was talking to me and that other people like Maria and Julia were tagging along and looking a bit jealous.

So I didn't go and find Riya and Gareth and Abhishek. And I didn't walk away from Seb, even though he had been mean to Aidan.

And I'm really sorry about that now. I don't really know how it all got nasty so quickly after Aidan admitted being at the demonstration, Dad. I think it had to do with Seb and his family. Chloe told us Aidan and Seb had gone to primary school together.

'Apparently Aidan Brocklesby was a show-off then, too,' said Chloe. 'Always winning things and stuff. Nobody else had a chance.'

'It's not Aidan's fault that he's good at things,' said Nola. 'I think Seb sounds as if he is jealous.'

After Miss Potter asked Aidan to give that amazing climbing display for us, Seb really seemed to have even more of a grudge against him. He couldn't stand the fact that Miss Potter had told him to watch and learn from Aidan. He just wouldn't let it go. He was always glaring at Aidan, or turning his back on him when he came into a room. It didn't help that Riya and Gareth and Abhishek went to Mrs Opie about Seb pushing Aidan in the corridor, and so Seb got detention. He totally deserved it, but he didn't seem to be sorry at all.

At first, Aidan didn't react to the little digs Seb kept making – 'oh dear, you look a bit pale and scared today' or 'everyone, keep the noise down, you're scaring Aidan' – and it looked like it would fizzle out, and things would just go on as normal at school. Like later that week, when our football team won against St Columba's. Aidan scored the winning goal, and everybody cheered him.

But then, the day after, I saw Seb talking to Tyler Lambert at break, and looking over at Aidan. It made me feel uneasy, because Seb and Tyler weren't normally friends, and everyone knew that Tyler Lambert was cross because he had tried to get into the football team but didn't. In the queue at lunch, Tyler came up to Aidan and said, 'I hear you and your parents say that soldiers are murderers. Are you saying my brother is a murderer?'

'No. That's not what I am saying,' said Aidan.

'What are you saying, then?' said Tyler, and he pushed Aidan so that his tray fell on the floor.

'Hey!' said one of the dinner ladies and, of course, Aidan and Tyler ended up going to Mrs Opie's office, and Tyler got detention.

I couldn't help thinking that made one more enemy for Aidan.

'So, school. Is it going OK?' said Dad, serving up the meal.

I went for Answer B.

'Yeah, pretty much,' I replied.

Chapter Nine

'You've chosen all your GCSEs?' asked Dad, as we started to eat. 'I know you chose art. Is it too much to hope you chose history too, in the end?'

'Yeah. I've chosen history. Me and Riya are going to be in the same group.'

Well, we were. I don't know what is going to happen now. The row we ended up having was so bad she might ask to change.

'Great.'

Dad didn't seem to know what to say next either.

We ate a bit more in silence.

'So . . . I'm going to give myself some time off tomorrow. Spend a bit of quality time with my daughter. Maybe we could visit the priory together? Or the castle?' said Dad. 'I realize this isn't much fun for you. Here on your own. With me. But hopefully we'll get you back home soon. Don't despair, Olivia.'

He gave me a smile. I tried to smile back. I knew I wasn't making things very easy for him, but it just felt so odd being miles away from home. And thinking about what has happened at school made me sad, and it all ran in together with Mum being arrested. I'd lost my appetite.

'Sorry,' I said, pushing the plate away. 'It's very nice, Dad, but I just . . .'

'No, no, it's fine, Olivia. Don't worry.' Dad cleared the plates away. 'Maybe you'll feel like some ice cream. Just to keep your energy levels up. I've got chocolate – your favourite. And chocolate flakes. I thought I'd push the boat out. No expense spared!' He opened the freezer.

Stan yawned and stretched, shook himself, then padded over and sat down next to me, putting his head on my lap. I knew he wasn't supposed to bother me at the table, but it was comforting to feel him leaning against me and to stroke his silky fur. His tail thumped at the floor, giving him away.

'Stan!' said Dad.

'I like him here,' I said. 'Please let him stay.' My voice sounded more pleading than I expected it to.

'Well, you're lucky Olivia is so soft,' Dad said to Stan.

Stan thumped his tail again, but didn't move his head from my knee. He was being a very good comfort dog.

'I think you're a bit soft too,' I said. 'Grandad says you should be stricter with him.'

Dad stiffened a little. I got the feeling I had hurt him, and I wasn't sure why. I wasn't sure what to say to put it right.

'You're all right, lad, aren't you? You don't need to go to dog boot-camp,' he said to Stan, and sat down opposite me, pushing my bowl towards me. Dad had put two flakes in my ice cream. One in his. It was sweet. Like I was little again and we were having a father-daughter treat.

'Thanks, Dad,' I said.

'That's OK,' said Dad, tucking into his ice cream.

Stan's tail thumped again.

'Olivia, I know you are worried about your mum being in a police cell, but really, she is an amazing person,' said Dad. 'If anyone can cope with this, she can. She's always so . . . positive. I know I got cross with her, but basically your mum is incredible. She is a very good and a very unusual person, and she will get through this.'

I realized I'd never really heard Dad praise Mum

like that before. I knew Gran had told me he was in love with my mum, but I'd never talked to Dad about it. He had never told me why they got together in the first place. What he saw in her.

'I know,' I said. 'I just feel a bit . . .' I wasn't even sure how worried I was about Mum. A bit of me was worried. Of course it was. I loved her. She was my mum, after all. But a bit of me wasn't. It was like, because I couldn't see it, I could pretend it wasn't happening. It was all very strange.

'It'll be easier when she has her hearing on Monday. I'm sure they will let her out then and you can go home. Look, I'm sorry about being grumpy earlier about work. It's good to have time with you, Olivia. We don't have enough time together on our own. We'll walk Stan — we'll be tourists together. My research can wait.'

I felt ridiculously pleased Dad wanted to spend time with me. I hadn't thought it would mean so much.

Dad's mobile rang.

'Hello? Yes. Is she OK? Good. OK. So, she is definitely being kept in police custody until Monday, and then hopefully we can arrange bail with the court? Right, so you'll keep me posted? Thanks.

Yes, of course, I'll pass you on to Olivia.'

Dad handed me the phone. 'It's Johnny,' he said.

It was odd hearing Johnny's voice while sitting at a table in a big airy kitchen on Lindisfarne, looking out through a window at the sky and the seabirds and the sea and the castle on the hill. To me, Johnny was about town, and our small kitchen.

'Hi, Olivia,' he said. 'Your mum is fine. I just wanted to let you and your dad know. I'll tell you what is happening as I find out, but basically we'll know more on Monday.'

'Is she . . . Is she OK?' I said.

'Yes, she's fine. Worried about you, of course, Olivia. I wanted to ring and check on you for her. Tell her I've spoken to you. It's good you're with your dad while she is in prison. Well, in police custody.'

It all seemed like a bad dream. I just held the phone and couldn't find any words to say. Dad came over and took it off me.

'Johnny? Hi. Look, thanks for keeping us informed. Stay in touch. Thanks. Bye.'

I sat down and put my head in my hands and burst into tears.

'Look, I really think the courts have better things to do than lock up your mum for making a hole in a fence and putting a flower in it. It was a piece of theatre to make a political point,' said Dad. 'Don't cry, love. There is nothing we can do at the moment.'

I lifted my head and Stan immediately moved in and tried to lick the salty tears from my cheeks.

'She's an adult,' said Dad calmly. 'She'll be all right, Olivia. It is absolutely no good worrying. We know where she is, we know she is safe, and she is with Sister Mary, who I believe is an old hand at this. Let's try not to worry. Now, how about taking Stan out for a quick walk before we settle down for the evening, and maybe find something to watch on the telly? I think this house has some DVDs we might like.'

To be honest, I wasn't sure if Dad and I shared the same taste, but I appreciated the thought.

He helped me up and gave me a quick hug around the shoulders. It was really nice, and sort of unexpected. Dad felt like, well, he felt like a proper dad. Confident, like Grandad. I didn't normally see Dad take charge of things. When I saw him at Gran and Grandad's he was different. I suppose there he acted more like their son. I know this might sound strange, and I know he teaches at a university and everything, but here he suddenly felt like a grown-up. More grown up than me. And it was nice. A relief.

We found the lead for Stan, and set off. Stan wagged his tail and was so excited to be going out again that it made me smile a bit.

I don't think I have ever met anyone who enjoys walking down a path more than Stan. He doesn't worry about anything – he just lives in the present.

I'd like to be more like Stan.

Chapter Ten

It was good to get out. Somehow, hearing the seagulls crying overhead and smelling the fresh sea air made me feel a bit better. I don't know why. I suppose it was all so different. Our town's only famous for its army base, and it's not even pretty, like Gran and Grandad's village.

I saw the castle on the skyline again. It felt like I had to keep looking at it, like it wanted me to pay attention to it.

'Why is Lindisfarne called Holy Island too? Why does it have a castle and a priory and everything? I mean, people on the mainland can't even get to them some of the time,' I asked.

'Actually, the Christian monks set up a very important monastery here in the seventh century, because travelling by boat then was safer than travelling by land,' said Dad. 'There were robbers and all sorts on land.'

'So is the monastery why you want to come and work here, then?' I said. I realized I didn't really know what Dad was researching. Somehow, I hadn't thought of him studying monks.

'Actually, no. I'm more interested in the castle,' said Dad.

We turned and walked around the village until we were back on the shore road leading up to the castle. I found myself looking over at the rocks to see if the boy had come back again, but he wasn't there.

'So is the castle medieval too?' I asked.

'Are you really interested, Olivia?' said Dad. 'I don't want to bore you. If I start talking about my work I might not be able to stop!'

'No, I really am,' I said. Because I was. Because I liked that Dad and I were having a proper conversation on our own, and I could see Dad lit up and enthusiastic about history. I'd sort of got into the habit of thinking people only got enthusiastic about doing things, like Mum, or believing in things, like Grandad. This was different. I liked it.

Dad unclipped Stan's lead and threw a ball up the deserted path to the castle. It felt like the island was ours. Up by the castle, I could see a couple walking, but there was nobody else around. Stan ran ahead to get the ball, happily bringing it back and dropping it at Dad's feet, ready for him to throw again.

'The great thing about this is that Stan runs at least three times the distance of our walk when I throw a ball,' said Dad. 'I'm hoping he will be properly tired out for the rest of the evening.' Stan set off again after the ball, his tail wagging with excitement.

'The original castle was built in Tudor times,' Dad continued, 'and was used as a garrison for soldiers, and after that as a coastguard station, but then it became a ruin. I'm writing about the castle before and during the First World War, when an American called Edward Hudson bought it and got it renovated.'

'So who owns it now?' I said.

'The National Trust.'

We had reached the gate at the top of the hill. Beyond it was a field and a sign for the spirally path up to the castle itself. We stood and looked up at it, towering above us.

Lindisfarne Castle itself is right on the top of a huge rocky hill, looking out to sea. It's not like a delicate fairy-tale castle – this castle was built for protection. It looks strong, built on its rock – strong against cold winds and bad weather; strong against wars if need be. I liked it.

'Did Edward Hudson give it to the National Trust, then?' I said.

'Not exactly. It's quite sad really. Edward Hudson never married, although he was once engaged to a famous cellist. She even gave concerts at the castle. Edward Hudson had no children, but quite a few families and friends' children came to stay over the years, because the air is so fresh and clean here. Anyway, one particular lad, Billy Congreve, came to stay, and loved the island and the birds and the wildlife so much that Edward Hudson decided to leave Lindisfarne Castle to him in his will.'

'And so, what happened? Why is it sad?'

'Well, the First World War came, and Billy went away to fight. And got killed. Won a medal for bravery and everything. But, obviously, he never got to inherit Lindisfarne Castle.'

'So, did Edward Hudson leave it to someone else?'

'No, I think he lost heart and sold it on – and eventually it was left to the National Trust.'

'I think people can stay there now, can't they?' I said. 'I met a boy on the beach earlier – he said he was staying at the castle.'

'Really? I didn't see that in the National Trust handbook,' said Dad. 'I think there's a residential flat for a warden, so maybe they are branching out and making holiday accommodation. You can stay in all sorts of amazing National Trust houses these days. I wish I'd known about staying at the castle. That would have been fantastic. Maybe I should ask about renting it another time. We could go up there tomorrow if you like.'

'OK, I'd like that,' I said.

Dad looked really pleased. As if I'd given him a present. But you could see he didn't want to go over the top, so he covered it up quickly.

'Right. I think we'll turn back now, so Stan can still have a run down the hill before we head home. I'll make some pancakes to go with the DVD.'

Dad smiled at me and I smiled back, and it felt good. Dad didn't get much chance to cook for me at Gran and Grandad's – it felt like he was making up for lost time!

A herring gull hovered and mewed above us, its white under-feathers pink from the setting sun. As we walked back down towards the village, I could see the moored boats floating by the shore and the lights coming on in the buildings – the pub at the corner, the holiday cottages, the farm. It was so quiet and beautiful, this island. It felt like another world, another time; like I could have dreamt Mum ending up in a police cell. All that was happening in the world was the sky and the sea and the birds, and Dad and me walking down a hill as Stan charged up and down it. I could almost have believed that all the trouble with Aidan had never happened, that there were no people at school to worry about, no protests about wars, no politics and no secrets to hide.

Chapter Eleven

Dad knocked on my door in the morning and I opened my eyes to a strange new bedroom. I was in a different space and it took me a few minutes to remember why I was there. We'd ended up having a really nice evening the night before. We'd kept off politics or Mum or anything difficult. Dad had told me more about the history of Lindisfarne: about all the medieval saints who had lived there and the little rocky island which one of them – St Cuthbert – used to pray on, and how you can walk over to it when the tide is right. We'd watched a couple of episodes of what Grandad calls a 'classic comedy' – *Dad's Army*. It's about the Home Guard during the Second World War – all these men preparing to defend Britain if the Nazis invaded, and it's really funny. I remember watching it with Mum and Grandad and Gran when I was little. Even Mum loved it. I suppose nobody gets killed in that programme. We had eaten pancakes, and I'd read a bit of the Lindisfarne guidebook in bed, but had fallen asleep really quickly.

The curtains were closed and the room was still dark, but I could see daylight coming through a gap in the curtains. I looked at my phone to check the time.

10 a.m. I'd slept for ages!

'Are you awake, Olivia?' Dad said, outside the door. 'I thought I'd let you lie in for a bit, but I wondered if you would like breakfast now? Then we could get ready and visit the castle.'

'OK,' I said, pulling my jumper on over my pyjamas. I pulled back the heavy curtains. It looked as if it was going to rain. The new day was grey. The clouds were being pushed around the sky by the wind, and the sea out past the moored fishing boats was dark, with white-tipped waves. I could see people in random groups of two or three making their way up the road to the castle. A black-headed seagull fought to hover in the air, riding the currents. It wasn't like the postcards, but it was beautiful. I knew that, miles away, Mum was alone, and locked up, and it felt weird that I was here . . . and that I didn't feel as bad as I thought I would about me being in a nice place while Mum was having a bad time.

Stan opened his eyes and wagged his tail when I got downstairs, but didn't bother to get out of his basket.

'I've taken him out for a long walk already,' said Dad. 'I left a note on the table in case you came downstairs and worried, but I had a feeling you would need a good sleep.'

We had toast and tea, I got dressed, and we set off up to the castle again. There were already a few people ahead of us on the road.

'I like the way the castle sort of looks down on everything, like it's part of the rocks and the island,' I said.

'Edwin Lutyens would have been pleased to hear you say that,' said Dad. 'He was the architect who worked on it for Edward Hudson when it was practically a ruin. He did a great job restoring it. He even got a famous garden designer called Gertrude Jekyll to make a garden up there – we'll go and see that too.'

We reached the top of the road and walked up the cobbled path from the bottom of the castle. It curved like a helter-skelter to the top. I looked down at the sea and tried to work out if the dark shapes bobbing among the waves were seals or not. I really wanted to see a seal.

When we got to the top, there were some wooden sheds. I thought whoever made them was really clever, as they reminded me of boats, but Dad said they *were* actually boats – traditional ones used by fishermen on Lindisfarne, which had been turned into sheds. Which was even more clever. Dad went into the office to buy our tickets. I stayed outside and felt the wind against my face.

I look down on the fields and see the boy in the long coat from the day before, walking across towards the castle. My hand goes up and I wave before I can stop myself, and I'm relieved that he didn't seem to see me. I feel myself blushing.

I was glad Dad came out with the tickets a moment later.

We went into the entrance hall and I loved it immediately. It reminded me of a cathedral, with its stone columns, and over a big fireplace there was what I thought at first was a beautiful painting on a wall, of a map with ships and a sea. Then I saw a metal needle or clock hand attached to the surface of the painting and thought it must be an unusual clock, or a compass or something, but it turned out to be neither. It was a wind indicator, connected to the weathervane on the roof – with a real, not a painted arrow – to show the direction of the wind outside. The arrow moved as I watched it, squeaking a little. I really liked it – I liked the colours and the ships and the green island in the middle. It reminded me of book illustrations, like the ones in the Narnia stories Gran and Grandad gave me.

'I'd love to paint something like that!' I said.

Dad laughed. 'Maybe offer to paint one for the vicarage then – I could imagine your grandad being delighted with one! This was painted in 1912,' he went on. 'It's hard to believe that it's over a hundred years old.'

Dad bought me a guidebook and we ambled around the castle. I loved it. It's so old, and just the way a castle should be – with thick walls built of stone, and little passages, and steps up and down where you don't expect them. It was good going around with Dad. He let me walk at my own pace and read each of the signs. I really liked the way they had set out the rooms as if frozen at the time of Edward Hudson. He had loads of visitors – even the man who wrote *Peter Pan* – J.M. Barrie – and Siegfried Sassoon, the First World War poet who we learnt about when we went on the First World War battlefield trip to Menin Gate in Ypres in Belgium, at the beginning of Year Nine.

There were quite a few other visitors looking around. I noticed a mum and dad who were really into the castle, with a bored-looking girl a bit younger than me and wearing headphones, who definitely wasn't. There were quite a few couples, including an elderly one who reminded me of Gran and Grandad, and a woman with a really sweet baby on her back – the baby smiled at me as her mum stood and looked at things. Following the guidebook, I started up the stairs to the top gallery.

Then I hear the music. It sounds so close, as if someone is playing the cello just above me, and my heart sort of twists inside me. It makes me think of missing Mum, and sadness and longing, but it's so beautiful that I want to hear more and see the performance.

I rush up the last few stairs to the gallery – but there's nobody there, and the music stops.

'Hello!' said Dad, coming up behind me. 'You raced on!'

'I wanted to hear the music. It was good, wasn't it?' I said.

'What music?' said Dad.

'The cello music.'

'There wasn't any music, Olivia,' said Dad. He looked at me very oddly. 'This *is* the long gallery where the cellist Madame Suggia played, though.'

'It must have been a recording then. It was wonderful.'

'Hmm,' said Dad, which really irritated me. He clearly didn't know me well enough. I wasn't someone who went around imagining music that's not there.

We walked back to the entrance hall. The woman at the desk gave me a very friendly smile and I decided to buy a postcard. As I was handing over the money, I asked, 'Do you have a CD of the music that was playing upstairs in the long gallery? Or can you tell me what it was?' I wanted Dad to hear, so I spoke loudly.

'Sorry. We weren't playing any music today,' said the woman.

'But . . . are you sure?' I said. Something was not right. 'I heard it as I was going up the stairs. It was really clear.'

'It must have been someone listening to music on headphones or something. Some people play their music far too loud. I know my grandson does. I always say to him, "Turn it down, Tom, you'll damage your ears."' She smiled as she handed me the bag with my postcard.

'I really did hear cello music,' I said to Dad as we walked home. I felt a bit embarrassed and cross. Dad was going to think I was imagining it, and I knew I wasn't. 'I don't understand it. There *was* a girl with headphones on, but what I heard wasn't second-hand. Maybe there was an audio guide or something playing in the room, but surely that woman would have known about it . . .'

Dad smiled at me and gave me a quick hug. 'Don't worry. Maybe there *was* a recording and one of the other staff was testing it and hadn't told her. It would be a good idea to play music up there.'

We walked back down the castle hill. It had got quite busy with people on the path now, and although it was still quite windy, the grey clouds had blown away, leaving blue sky and sun.

'I was thinking about lunch,' Dad said. 'How does homemade pizza sound? And then, after lunch, I should really get some work done.' When I didn't reply he asked, 'Are you feeling OK, Olivia?'

'About Mum? I'm worried, of course,' I said.

'Right. But you don't feel ill or anything? You just look a little . . . pale. That's all.'

'No. I'm fine,' I said. I did actually feel fine, and I loved the sea breeze. But I did feel a bit weird about the music.

Stan was really excited to see us when we got in. He was bouncing and wagging his tail, and generally getting in the way of Dad as he tried to sort out things for the pizza.

'I'll take him out if you like,' I said.

'That would be a big help – thanks, Olivia,' said Dad. 'I'll nip up to the village store and get some tomatoes for the topping, but it won't take long. Then I'll make the pizza and when you get back we'll pop it in the oven. You don't have to stay out that long. He's had a walk already. I don't want you getting overtired.'

'I'm fine, honestly I am,' I said, trying to get Stan

to stand still long enough for me to hook the lead on to his collar ring. I opened the door, and me and Stan erupted on to the path. You'd never have thought he had already had a long walk with Dad, as he panted his way forward, pulling me to the gate.

'Sit!' I said sternly, as I caught up with him and opened it. Stan sat, his tongue out, his tail sweeping the path. His eyes pleaded with me to go, and I laughed. He was so easy to understand. He didn't care about politics and he didn't make things complicated, the way people did. It was such a relief to be with him and have a break from all the mess back home.

Chapter Twelve

We swing out right, down to the main street, and then Stan pulls me left up towards the castle again. I should pull him back and make him walk to heel, but he seems to know where he wants to go and there doesn't seem any point fighting him. Nobody is around – the tide is in. Everyone seems to have got off the island really quickly, probably scared by the horror stories of people getting stranded in those towers because they crossed when it wasn't safe. Even the ice-cream van has gone.

A gull cries in the air. I unclip Stan's lead. He charges off at top speed up the hill and I see, too late, that he is heading towards a figure walking down it. Then I blow out my breath. It's the boy. William.

'Stan!' I call, and run as fast as I can after him. By the time I get there, William is sitting on the ground, Stan licking him.

'Sorry!' I say, grabbing Stan by the collar. 'Again!'

'Don't worry,' says William. He gets to his feet and dusts himself down. 'I wasn't expecting him, that's all. He seemed to come out of nowhere. He is a handsome dog. Maybe a bit headstrong, though?'

I laugh. I like the way he speaks, and the way he smiles at me as he says it. His words match the tweed jacket he is wearing and I like his style.

I see him looking at my shirt and trousers and Doc Marten boots, and he smiles too. 'So, Olivia, isn't it? I haven't seen you up at the castle yet.'

'I visited this morning with my dad,' I say.

'You were there with your father?' he says. 'I'm sorry I missed you. Is he an artist too?'

'Pardon?' I say, not sure if I have understood him properly.

'Believe me, nobody at the castle will have thought you strange. I like the artistic way you dress. Truly, I do.'

I look to check he is not being sarcastic or mean. but his face is so sincere. His eyes are so kind and honest that I can see he is trying to be nice, in an odd sort of way. He is what Gran calls 'well meaning'. He's just a little odd, but there's nothing nasty about him. Not like Seb.

Stan runs up to us with a stick, and William picks it up and throws it down to the beach. Stan charges after it and runs across the sand.

'So *is* your father an artist?' he says.

'No, he's a lecturer at Durham University.'

'Ah! Like Sir Oliver Lodge, the famous physicist. He's a professor at Birmingham. He is visiting the castle at the moment. They should meet.'

Stan charges back, covered with sand. He drops the stick at William's feet and William throws it long and far, as we continue down the hill.

'You're good at that,' I say.

'I'd hope so. I was captain of the cricket team last year. Before I got ill.'

'What was the matter?' I say.

'You're direct, aren't you?' He smiles. 'Diphtheria. Rotten, as you know.'

I don't really know, but he seems to think I do. He might think I am being too direct if I ask what exactly diphtheria is, so I don't.

'I'm sorry,' I say.

'Oh, I was lucky. I pulled through,' he says, as Stan comes panting back with the stick. William picks it up and throws it again. 'Some chaps end up with a weak heart, or paralysis. Some even die. I'm strong. No lasting side effects. Thanks to Lindisfarne. The doctor said I needed sea air and rest, so I got sent here. It did the trick. And it's beautiful. How about you? Why are you here?'

'My dad has rented a house for the summer. He has to work.'

I hope he won't ask about my mum. He doesn't.

We reach the turning and he goes to walk on but suddenly I think of something.

'William, I'm sure I heard cello music up at the castle this morning, but nobody else seems to have heard it. You're staying there – have you heard it?'

'Often,' says William. 'Of course.'

'Oh, good!' I say. 'I'll tell Dad. I think he thought I was hearing things.'

'Hasn't he heard of Madame Suggia?' William says. He sounds surprised.

'Yes, but I thought what I heard wasn't a recording,' I begin, but I hear Stan barking furiously and I glance back to see he has somehow managed to get himself tangled up in something – maybe some netting or something from the fishing boats. Some fisherman must have been drying it in the sun.

'Stan!' I yell. He is barking loudly and urgently

now, and I run back down the road to him, before he hurts himself or damages whatever he is caught up in.

'Sorry!' I shouted back over my shoulder, but William had walked on and was nowhere to be seen.

Chapter Thirteen

Stan was just as pleased to go home as to go out for the walk, and an indignant blackbird flew off in alarm as we hurtled down the path.

'Hi. Everything all right?' Dad said, as we walked into the kitchen. He was wearing a blue and white striped apron, and kneading dough. The table was laid already: glasses and cutlery on the clean, bare wood, the jug full of water, a bowl of green salad and some salad dressing beside it.

It was all much more organized than when Mum serves meals. She isn't great at timing, and when dinner is ready her table is still nearly always, always covered with piles of paper and books and pens and sketched-out plans for garden designs or agendas for meetings. I am always the emergency table clearer. It drives me mad, as there isn't really anywhere to put anything but on a chair or on the floor, so they always end up being put back on the table when the meal is over.

'Fine.'

'You were away a while. Did you go far?'

'Not really. I met that boy who is staying up at the castle. Stan jumped at him and knocked him over, but he was really nice about it.'

'Oh no. Bad dog, Stan,' said Dad.

Stan was completely oblivious to Dad's words. He sat as if waiting for a treat, his tail swishing across the stone floor.

Dad tutted.

I passed Stan a chew toy and he padded over with it to his basket, curving himself round and promptly going to sleep.

'Well, the pizza should be ready in quarter of an hour or so,' Dad said.

'OK, I'll go up to my room, then,' I said.

'Fine. I'll call you when it's ready,' said Dad.

I checked my phone. No texts. I didn't want to look at anything else. Certainly not any group chats. They had been horrible about Aidan on so many of them. What were they going to say about Mum, now she had been arrested? News spreads quickly. Maybe Chloe would know by now. What would her family say? I couldn't bear more people being angry. I felt my stomach churn a little just remembering.

I got out my sketchbook to draw the view from the window, but found my head too full. The page stayed blank.

'Pizza's ready!' Dad called, and I went downstairs.

Dad didn't ask me anything more about William as I sat down. If I had told Mum I had been chatting to a boy, she would have made too big a deal of it – she would have been bursting to ask me more about him. That's why I hadn't told her about me and Aidan climbing together. Not that it was an issue any more, of course. Aidan would never want to climb with me again. Dad was more focused on lunch, so I escaped any embarrassing questions, or the loaded, hopeful are-you-going-to-share-things-with-me silence that Mum was so good at.

He put two slices on each of our plates, slid the pizza tray and slicer in the sink, hung up his apron and sat down.

'I think this is going to be rather good, if I say so myself,' he said proudly.

I took a slice of pizza and bit into it. The taste exploded in my mouth – it was perfect, just the right temperature, and with the cheese melting into the herby tomato sauce.

'It's really delicious, Dad,' I said. He looked so pleased, and that made me feel good. It really mattered to him that I liked his pizza, and it suddenly really mattered to me that he knew I did. Plus, I really *did* like the pizza, so it was win-win! It wasn't hard to make him happy.

Stan padded over and sat beside me, his head on my knee, his eyes appealing to me.

'No feeding Stan at the table,' said Dad, and Stan obviously understood, as he gave a big sigh and went to lie under it.

Dad had made salad dressing and put it in a little jug, and I dribbled some over the lettuce.

That's the sort of thing Johnny does when he cooks meals. Mum is a salad-cream girl. She said that her mum had always given them salad cream as a treat. She never says much else about her mum or dad. She said things weren't good for her growing up, and she'd tell me about it more one day, but it hasn't happened yet. I've never even met my other grandparents. I don't even know if they are alive. Family is me and Mum and Gran and Grandad and Dad and Stan.

Gran and Grandad met Mum before Dad did. Mum left home and turned up at the church youth group, saying she was staying in a hostel. She was only sixteen, but Gran said she was full of opinions and ideas even then. Gran and Grandad liked her straight away. Gran said it was impossible not to love her. And when Dad – shy, studious Dad – met her at the youth group, he obviously felt the same.

'Dad. You know you and Mum . . .?' I said. 'Do you think . . . Would you like to . . . Do you think you will ever get back together? I mean, I know it's ages . . . years ago . . . since you were . . . but . . . ' I tailed off as Dad shook his head.

'Why are you asking me this now, Olivia?' he said gently.

'I don't know. I suppose . . . you said she was . . . you said she is an amazing person.'

'She is. Your mum *is* amazing, Olivia. Beautiful, clever, unique. And I really loved her. I *do* really love her. But we just aren't right for each other. She realized that quicker than me. She never wanted to marry me. I was really hurt. And mixed up . . . especially when you came along. I wanted to stay together with you so much, Olivia. I think that all got mixed up with being with your mum. But not any more. Not for ages now. Years and years.'

'Gran thinks you've never got over her. That you're still sad about it all.'

Dad sighed and ran his fingers through his hair. It made it stand up a little, and he looked more like the pictures of him as a schoolboy. 'Gran is wrong. The thing I'm sad about is missing seeing you grow up, not living with you as your dad. I think . . .' He looked at me and frowned, as if he was choosing his words very carefully. He started slowly but then the words rushed out of him. 'Your gran and grandad . . . Your gran and grandad meant well, but perhaps I shouldn't have let myself be elbowed out of your life. I was only seventeen, and I felt as if your grandad knew more about being a dad than me, and I think he felt that way too. So, even though I was living with you when you were born, it felt like sometimes you already had three parents – your mum and your gran and your grandad – and they all seemed to want me to go away. They all seemed to want me to go away,' he repeated, and looked really sad.

My heart felt sore just listening to him; just looking at him with his sticky-up hair. He must have felt so bad. I'd never heard Dad talk about his feelings like this before.

'Nobody wanted me to be your dad, but me. They all wanted me to be more like your big brother than your father – to cuddle you and entertain you but not make any decisions about your life or take responsibility. I can understand. Your gran and grandad felt I was too young, and your mum didn't want to be stuck with me. But I wish I had fought them more, spoken about what I wanted – needed – too. I wish I had listened to what I wanted, and then had stuck to my guns.'

'But Mum stayed with me,' I said. 'Mum didn't go away.' I felt mean, like I was sticking the knife in, but I needed to say it. It was true. Dad winced.

'I know. I'm sorry, Olivia. Your mum . . . Your mum is your mum. Nobody could tell her who she was. But I wasn't as strong as her. I wasn't as sure. I'm sorry. I regret that.'

I had never imagined this. I thought Dad was happy just visiting me and getting on with his life. And he was right. I thought of Grandad more as a dad than him. Like with everything that had happened since Easter – it was Grandad, not Dad, I had told about my problems joining the cadets. It was Grandad who Mum had argued with. Did Dad even know about what had gone on at school? About

Aidan and his parents and the stuff in the news – in the papers and online, and how horrible it had all become? I hadn't told him – had anyone?

Maybe it was time to tell him. Dad had just said he wished he had been around more, had been more of a dad. He seemed so much more . . . It sounds strange, especially since I'd just seen a glimpse of the worried boy he was at school – but here on Lindisfarne, he seemed more like a dad. He was more grown-up, away from the vicarage. It would be a relief to ask his advice.

'Dad,' I started. 'It's been a bit awful at school since Easter. Everyone has fallen out and . . .'

'It's not as if I don't love my job, Olivia,' Dad said at the same time. 'Sorry, Olivia. Were you saying something?'

'No, you first,' I said. I suddenly felt so glad I was with Dad, that I really was important to him, and had always been, and that we were talking together, sharing things properly on our own, without Mum and Gran and Grandad there. Maybe, I thought, if I could just tell him everything that had happened with Aidan, he could help make sense of it. That was his job, after all. He once told me that being a historian meant he took the past and looked at all the different points of views and facts, and tried to find out as much of the truth as he could. Maybe he could help me. Help Aidan.

'Well, I just wanted to say that I do love my job and living in Durham,' said Dad. 'And . . . I wasn't sure how or when to tell you this, but since you asked me about getting back together with your mum . . . I've been meaning to tell you, Olivia. I have met someone. A woman . . . Her name is Alice. She's another lecturer at the university. I met her first in America, but now she is working in Durham too, in the art history department. And . . . she's lovely, Olivia. I would like to marry her. I really want you to meet her soon.'

I didn't know what to say. Just when I felt I was getting closer to Dad, that I was important to him, he did this. I felt pushed away again, like Alice was the one he really wanted to spend time with, not me. I thought I was getting to know him, that we could catch up on lost time. Get to know each other. I could tell him about school. And now it had turned out he was more interested in someone else. Someone new. This Alice. There wouldn't be any time for me. No time alone. There was never any time for me or my problems. Nobody cared about my point of view or was totally on my side. And it hurt. My heart hurt.

'I need to go for a walk, Dad. I need to think,' I said. I couldn't wait to get away. I'd only wanted to talk to Dad about what was happening with Aidan, not have a whole new thing to think about. Dad and this Alice woman . . . Another mum.

Stan got up out of his basket and wagged his tail, totally not getting the mood. I rushed past him, out of the kitchen into the hallway, and put my shoes on. Stan was beside me, getting in the way, eager to go for another walk, but I pushed him back in as I opened the door.

'Olivia, don't go!' Dad followed me too. 'I'm sorry. I shouldn't have just blurted it all out like this. Let's sit down and talk more. You wanted to tell me something. Let me hear what you wanted to say.'

'I'm sorry, Dad, I've just got to have a bit of space,' I said. And I closed the door on both of them.

Chapter Fourteen

I strode down the path, startling a little group of sparrows into the air, and let the gate swing shut behind me.

I didn't feel like going towards the sea and the castle again. I felt like doing something different, so I turned by the Ship Inn and the Lindisfarne Scriptorium, and headed past the National Trust shop and some other gift shops.

I thought everyone had gone, but as I stomped down the street the shops were all still open and there seemed to be so many more people about than when I had been talking to William. There was a little boy crying and asking to go and buy fudge, and people looking in windows at Celtic jewellery. I saw the couple and the bored-looking girl who had been up at the castle walking down the street, licking ice creams. The girl looked much happier now. People were sitting in the cafes, and waiting outside shops with dogs. It was all a bit too busy. I needed to be somewhere other people weren't.

I wasn't really sure where I was heading, so I kept walking until I got right to the end of the street, past a little garden and kept going.

The tide was out, and people were walking across the shore over to a little bit of land in the sea. The place Dad says they call St Cuthbert's Island. I wondered if William was there. But I didn't really want to have to talk to anyone and I didn't want to go back to the house and face Dad.

I felt a bit bad about walking out on Dad and not being nicer to him about Alice. I felt bad about Mum. I felt bad about Aidan and school, and horrible about the mess with cadets. I felt bad about everything. I suddenly really wanted to cry, but I wasn't ready to go home – or rather, back to the holiday house. I saw a sign for St Mary's Church and thought I would try to find somewhere quiet to sit there, and just get my head around things. The tourists would be busy in the shops or visiting the priory or castle, or having their photos taken with the birds of prey. There was even a film crew filming some people down by the beach for the BBC or something. Nobody would be in the church.

So I walk to the church and push open the door, and I have only taken a few steps inside before I realize that there is a church service going on. They are singing Grandad's favourite hymn, 'Jerusalem'.

> 'And did those feet in ancient times,
> Walk among England's mountains green?
> And was the Holy Lamb of God,
> On England's pleasant pastures seen?'

Except it isn't a real church service. They must be filming here as well – a documentary or something – because I can see all the people in the pews to my right, and everyone is in Edwardian costume. I feel really embarrassed. The television company should have put warning signs outside. Luckily all the people pretending to be in the service have their backs to me and nobody seems to have noticed. The women, in their lovely Edwardian feathered hats, and the smartly dressed men keep staring ahead, and the organ keeps playing as they sing.

'*And did the countenance divine,*
Shine forth upon our clouded hills?
And was Jerusalem builded here,
Among these dark satanic mills?'

I suddenly notice William there – one of the extras singing in the congregation. With his tweed jacket he fits right in. His voice is really strong and loud, and he sounds like he really means every word he is singing.

'*Bring me my bow of burning gold;*
Bring me my arrows of desire:
Bring me my spear: O clouds unfold!
Bring me my chariot of fire!'

I walk backwards to the door, hoping nobody will suddenly leap out at me and some director or someone will yell 'CUT!' in a cross voice. I seem to have got away with it, and I close the door as they get to the last verse.

'*I will not cease from mental fight,*
Nor shall my sword sleep in my hand:
Till we have built Jerusalem,
In England's green and pleasant land.'

The door closed shut and I couldn't hear the singing any more. All I could hear was the mewing of a seagull above me, flying out to sea, and the mixed calls of sparrows chirping and a blackbird whistling. It was time to go back. The fresh air and just getting away for ten minutes had cleared my head. Maybe even the hymn. It reminded me of Grandad, and home, and Dad. He had grown up in Grandad's world, singing the hymns Grandad chose for him to sing, meaning every word. I suddenly felt as if I knew just what it had been like for him as a seventeen-year-old boy, the vicar's gentle son with his pregnant girlfriend. Trying so hard to do the right thing. He wasn't like Mum or Grandad, who are naturally and passionately sure of what to do, about what is right and what is wrong. He is gentle and sensitive and a bit anxious. And he loved me. He had loved me then and he loved me now. And if he had met someone nice, why shouldn't he be happy?

I felt in my pocket. The twenty pounds Dad gave me was still in it. I'm not old enough to buy him a treat from the Lindisfarne mead shop, but Dad likes fudge too, so I walked back to Pilgrims Fudge Kitchen and bought Dad some coffee and cream flavour. There wasn't any dog-friendly fudge, but I decided that I'd take Stan out again to show him I was sorry I hadn't brought him with me this time. At least I was definitely going to get fit that weekend!

So I walked back to the house and pushed open the door. Stan rushed up to me, waving his tail, and gave me a lick. He wasn't offended at all. I love that about dogs. They are very forgiving.

Dad wasn't in the kitchen. I could hear his voice, though, and I realized he was on the phone in the sitting room next door.

'I've blown it, I think, Alice.'

I stopped by the door. His back was to me. I stepped to the side so he wouldn't notice me. I knew I shouldn't be eavesdropping, but I guessed he was talking about me to Alice, so I felt like I had the right. She was going to be my step-mum, after all.

'It was too much for her. I don't know what I was thinking. I've kept quiet about it all her life and now . . . I'm so frustrated with myself.'

There was a pause, then he continued, 'Oh, I hope so, Alice. Talking with you the other night really made me see things more clearly. I wanted to explain, let her know I didn't just abandon her. I wanted to tell her how much I loved her – *love* her – and want to be her dad, but I blurted it all out much too fast. She couldn't get away from me quickly enough.' He sounded so miserable.

'Dad,' I said.

He turned round, eyes wide for a moment. 'I've got to go, Alice. I'll ring you later. Thanks,' he said hurriedly, and ended the call.

We stood there, looking at each other – me in the doorway, him standing by the other door.

'I've bought you some fudge,' I said, showing him the bag.

'Oh, Olivia,' he said. 'I'm so sorry I messed it up. I just wanted to tell you I loved you. I do love you, you know that, Olivia?'

'Yes. I know. I love you too,' I said. 'And I'm happy for you about Alice. Honestly. I'm glad you've met someone lovely. You deserve it. It was just a shock to hear about her so suddenly.'

He opened his arms a bit shyly, and I ran over to him and we gave each other a hug.

It felt good.

'I'm sorry about ruining the pizza lunch,' I said.

'I can warm it up, if you like.'

'That would be good,' I said. 'The bit I ate was delicious.'

So I sat at the table again, and I watched as Dad heated up the pizza. Stan came over and lay at my feet.

'Voila!' Dad said with a flourish, giving me my lunch again. I hadn't realized just how hungry I was until I ate it. It was just as delicious as the first time round – the melting cheese, the crisp bread. I looked out of the window and watched a seagull fly across the sky. Neither of us said anything. It felt like nothing needed to be said. There was no gap to be bridged, no awkward silence. Stan sighed happily, and put his head on his paws. Dad made coffee and cleared my plate and glass away into the dishwasher.

'I bought the Sunday paper this morning. I think I'll take my fudge and coffee and catch up a bit on the world's news, in the sitting room,' Dad said.

'I'd like the magazine bit,' I said.

I still had to talk to Dad about Aidan. I wanted to hear about this Alice too. But later. Not then, not when things were suddenly so good. I could keep all the rubbish things at a distance. Where they belonged. I just wanted to have a nice, uncomplicated time for once.

So we all three got up and went into the sitting

room, and Dad and I settled down to eat fudge and read our bits of the paper while Stan stretched out and dreamt of rabbits, his paws twitching in his sleep.

Chapter Fifteen

I couldn't settle. I tried to be interested in what the younger royals do on holiday, and a recipe for cheesecake, but I couldn't manage it. Maybe, I thought, my approach wasn't working. Maybe I couldn't just distance myself from things when they were too difficult. Maybe I should tell Dad about things after all.

I looked up to talk to Dad, but all I could see were the headlines on the front of his newspaper: *Government Foil Terror Plot to Blow Up Tube Station. Terror Suspects on Run.* There was a picture of people crying, covered in blood, after a bombing somewhere in another country I hadn't heard of, which the people on the run were linked to. It just made me feel sad. Wars were horrible. Aidan and Mum were right about that. But Grandad and the other people in the army weren't saying wars were OK, just that they were always going to happen. And if we had to have them, we had to be prepared – which meant having well-trained soldiers to fight. I could understand that too.

Everyone was so sure of their opinions and nobody seemed to be prepared to look at what the other side thought. Not in the world, not in our family, not at school.

The week after Seb and Tyler both got detention for pushing Aidan, we had a special assembly. I felt really proud to see Grandad up on the stage in his army uniform.

Mrs Opie introduced him. 'I am very glad to say that Major Andrew Harvey has come to talk to us about his experiences in Afghanistan.'

I hadn't talked to Grandad about what was going on with Aidan. Or Mum, for that matter. I knew if I talked about Aidan being bullied, both Mum and Grandad would want to know the background to it, who was doing it and why. They would both want to know if the school knew, and what they were doing about it. Then the whole thing about arguments about pacifism and us having cadets at school would come out. Knowing Mum, she would be up to the school to protest about it before I could stop her, and I'd never be allowed to join. It wasn't a problem, Grandad knowing about cadets, of course, but I didn't really want him to know about Aidan not wanting to be in it and being on the protest with Mum. I don't know why. I suppose I just didn't want Grandad to think badly of him too. Like the others did. Aidan didn't deserve that.

'I'm delighted to be here today,' said Grandad, 'to tell you about the two vocations I have and how I feel they support each other – to be a Christian priest and to be a soldier.'

I realized I had never actually ever heard Grandad specifically talk about those two things. I mean, I knew he was a priest and a soldier, of course. At the Remembrance Day church service, it was clear he knew the soldiers who came in uniform to lay wreaths, but I'd never really thought about how the two parts of his life might link together.

It was a really good talk. Gran always says Grandad looks so distinguished in his uniform, and I know what she means. Grandad showed us lots of interesting photos. He talked about getting to know the local people where they were posted, and praying in the operating theatre when an injured soldier came in. He talked about being in a complex that came under fire, and how facing death had really deepened his faith. I saw Nola blink back tears, and I gave her hand a squeeze, but she was smiling too and listening really carefully to Grandad, so I think she was OK. Grandad talked about teamwork and selflessness and how much he had learnt from the bravery and loyalty of the other soldiers. He said how glad he was that the school was going to have its own army cadet corps, and how he would do what he could to support us.

'He's brilliant,' Chloe said, as we started out of the hall afterwards.

I felt so proud of him. I could see people looking at me admiringly.

'I can't wait to join the cadets,' said Nola. 'Have you talked to your Mum yet, Olivia? We have to have the permission slips in by the end of the week. I think they are going to order uniforms and stuff.'

That gave me an idea. I told them to go on ahead, and I hung back and caught Grandad before he left. He was talking to Mrs Opie, who was smiling and looking very pleased.

'Grandad, could you sign the permission slip for me to join the cadets? The deadline is soon and I don't want to miss the chance to sign up,' I said quickly, taking out the letter I'd had at the bottom of my bag since Major Lee had first come in to speak.

'Lovely!' said Mrs Opie. 'Good to see you following in the family tradition, Olivia! Let's have a photo of grandad and granddaughter.'

I felt a bit embarrassed, but I was concentrating on getting the slip done, so I posed with Grandad, then he signed the slip and I took it to the office.

It was such a relief, being able to hand it in! I knew I still had to talk to Mum, but September was ages away. I had time.

Or so I thought.

I didn't know that Mrs Opie would put the picture of us, and an article on Grandad's speech, on our school website that day, with a headline saying: *Student Follows Family Tradition and Joins the Cadets.*

Mum was furious. She was furious with the school, she was furious with Grandad, and she was furious with me.

'I had a phone call from the Brocklesbys to tell me to look at the school website. I can't believe it! Why didn't you tell me about this, Olivia?' she said at breakfast the next day. 'How dare they brainwash you like this? And how can they allow you to join up, anyway? I haven't seen any permission slips.'

'I asked Grandad to sign it,' I said quietly, but firmly.

'You did what?' Mum said. 'Olivia!'

'I knew you wouldn't agree,' I said. 'But I really want to do it. It looks fun, I think I'll be good at it, and I just want to be normal.'

'So you think it's normal to be in the army?' said Mum. 'You think it's normal to be trained to kill people?'

'That's so unfair,' I said. I refused to meet her eyes and get caught up in all the drama. 'You're just exaggerating. This is army *cadets*, not the army. Doing cadets doesn't mean I have to join the army. Most people who are in the cadets don't go on to be soldiers. And even if I did join the army, it isn't all about killing people. That's so typical of you. *That's* why I didn't tell you about it in the first place,' I said. 'You only see what you want to see.'

'And your grandad doesn't, I suppose?' said Mum. 'I'm so disappointed in you both. I've got to go to work now, but I'll talk about this more with you tonight.'

Later it was just the same conversation, the same arguments. And then it got worse. Mrs Opie had given the picture to the papers. There must not have been much happening locally that week, because a few days later it was all over the front page of the *Gazette*.

Chloe was really excited about it.

'Olivia! You're famous!' she said. She had put a copy of the *Gazette* on my desk.

'You should get that framed,' said Nola.

'You look lovely,' said Riya.

I tried to get caught up in their enthusiasm, but then I saw Seb's cousin from Year Twelve come in and talk to Seb. She looked over at Aidan. Seb said something and laughed. It wasn't a very nice laugh.

When she left, Seb went over to Aidan's desk, where he and Gareth and Abhishek were playing cards.

'So, Quaker Boy, my cousin says your mum and dad have started an online petition against our school having cadets,' he said.

'Yes,' said Aidan. 'Well, not just our school, it's any school.'

'Why?' said Chloe, who had overheard. She said it quite loudly, so that it caught other people's attention and they started drifting over.

'They don't think military cadet groups should be attached to schools, that's all. It makes it seem like a subject, like maths. It's making it too normal.'

'But it *is* normal – duh!' said Seb. 'How long have your parents been living in this town? This is an *army* town for army people. Not cowards.'

'My parents aren't cowards,' said Aidan, standing up.

'They don't want to fight our enemies – that's who I call cowards,' said Seb.

'Tell your parents to leave Olivia and her grandad alone,' said Chloe to Aidan.

I felt suddenly sick – I wasn't sure how she thought it had anything to do with us in particular.

'It's OK, Chloe,' I said. 'I don't mind.'

Aidan looked at me, frowning.

I knew I could have done better than that; that I could have stuck up for him more. But it was the fact I could see both sides which was the problem. I just worried that if I started to explain what pacifists thought, people might start thinking that – because I knew so much about it – I must feel the same, even if I told them I didn't. I wanted them to see that I felt like Grandad about cadets, not Mum or Aidan's parents or even Aidan. But somehow I didn't want to come out and say I definitely didn't agree with Mum and Aidan, because I didn't want to think about what Aidan would think of me then. Besides, it was just a petition. I knew all about them from living with Mum. A petition just meant one group of people wanted change and weren't afraid to sign their name to something in writing saying that, and to talk about it in public. That was all. It wasn't my petition. It wasn't my fight.

'His parents aren't being mean to Olivia, Chloe,' said Riya. 'They are just saying we shouldn't have military cadet groups *in schools*, that it isn't appropriate. That's the only issue this petition is about. You can still join the cadets out of school time. They're not trying to stop you doing that.'

I felt a bit ashamed that Riya was doing what I should have done – trying to get people to understand. But she hadn't had to put up with these arguments her whole life, like I had. School was the place I could take a break from all this. Usually.

'Why does it matter? Nobody's making Quaker Boy come to cadets,' said Seb, taking a step towards Aidan. 'He can go climbing on his own, when we are there.'

Gareth and Abhishek stood up next to Aidan,

facing Seb. I saw Tyler and Harry look over at them, their expressions like stone. The atmosphere in the classroom turned brittle. I was worried Tyler and Harry were going to come over and get involved and then the whole thing would get out of hand. But then Mr Amis came in to take the register, and everyone shut up and sat down in their places. Everything went quiet. A little too quiet. Except my heart. That was still thumping out of control.

Chapter Sixteen

I felt sick just remembering how close things had got to going so wrong that day. Thankfully, Dad didn't notice how quiet I had gone. He probably thought I was just relaxing. But these thoughts made me feel like I'd never be able to relax again. I'm not sure how much time passed, but I got up and told him I'd take Stan for a walk.

'Another one? Are you OK?' Dad said.

I just nodded, called Stan and headed out, before he could ask me anything more. It all felt too messy to talk about right then.

I'm glad the streets are quiet. I don't want to see happy tourists when I feel so bad, or have people wonder why I'm looking teary. Stan and I set off down the road towards the beach. I am miserably remembering school, when suddenly he gives an enthusiastic woof and startles me back to the present and Lindisfarne. He starts pulling on the lead – he has seen William, and I let him pull me over to where William is standing on his own, skimming stones across the water.

'Hello. You're good at that,' I say, coming up behind him. He jumps.

'Sorry, I didn't mean to startle you,' I say, as Stan pushes forward to have a fuss made of him. William laughs, and strokes his ears.

Since there's no one else here to get startled by an overenthusiastic red setter bounding up to them, I let Stan off the lead. He runs, nose down, sniffing his way across the grass bank, his tail waving madly; picking up the scents of all the people and dogs who have been there before.

'I saw you in church,' I say. 'It looked fun, everyone dressed up. Was it some *Songs of Praise* thing?'

I don't know what I have said wrong, but William looks really offended. 'Please don't talk about church like that. I've had enough of this up at the castle from the artistic visitors. That's why I came down here, to get away from it.'

I feel awful. Why do I keep upsetting people I like? First Aidan and Riya, now William.

'I'm sorry,' I say. 'I didn't mean it as a joke. I loved all the clothes people were wearing, and "Jerusalem" is my grandad's favourite hymn. He's a vicar. I don't go to church much, but I would never laugh at people who do. Honest, William, I didn't mean to hurt your feelings.'

He picks up another stone and skims it across the water. It bounces four times. I pick up a really nice flat one and throw it. It bounces four times too.

'Where did you learn that?' he says, throwing another – four times again.

'My grandad,' I say. I carefully choose an especially good-shaped pebble, and skim it. 'Five!' I say in triumph.

'I have never met a girl who can throw as well as me,' he says.

'You obviously don't know many girls then,' I reply. Honestly, he is nice, but a bit patronizing.

He laughs, and I breathe a sigh of relief that he doesn't seem offended any more.

'Look, a curlew,' I say. I love seeing it there with its long, curving bill, standing still on the beach. It's not a garden or town bird – it belongs to the sea and the sand. It's perfectly at home here, being itself. Unfortunately, Stan sees it too and lollops down the beach after it. It takes off, crying into the wind.

'I love that sound,' I say. 'I hear gulls at home, even though we are nowhere near the sea, but never curlews. I saw some sandpipers when we were arriving, and I think I've seen a plover. I'd really like to see some seals close up.'

'I saw some earlier, near St Cuthbert's.'

'I remember my grandmother saying you have to sing to seals,' I say.

'What would you sing?'

'I don't know. A sea song, I suppose. "Speed, Bonny Boat" or something.'

He laughs again and throws another stone.

'Five!' he says.

'Four!' I correct.

He picks up another and throws it.

'Now, that was five,' I say.

He seems satisfied.

'I think I'll walk back up to the castle now,' he says.

'I'll walk along with you, if that's OK?' I say.

'Of course. If you like, I could show you Miss Jekyll's garden on the way.' He says it a little shyly. 'I thought I might do some sketching there.'

'Yeah, that would be great. Thanks,' I say. 'Dad and I meant to go this morning, but we forgot. I'd like to do some drawing too.'

I call Stan and we walk to the top of the hill, where two little girls come rushing down towards us.

'William! Come and play with us!' says the older one. She looks about seven. Her hair is long and her Edwardian costume is a bit dirty. She must have been an extra in the church and then gone playing on the beach.

William laughs.

'Hello, Dora! As you can see, I'm with my friend, Olivia,' he says, pointing at me. 'We're going to the garden.'

The smaller girl laughs, as if he has said the funniest thing in the world. 'Can we come with you? *Please*, William?' she says, holding his hand.

'I'm not sure, I'll have to ask Olivia. We might be doing some drawing, and I'm not sure if you could stay quiet enough, Nessie.'

'But I said please like you taught me!' says Nessie, seeming very offended.

'What do you think, Olivia – shall we let them come?' says William, turning to me. He is nice to little kids. I like that about him.

Stan gives a sudden pull and his lead slips out of my hand. He rushes forward, wagging his tail, and the girls scream.

'Sorry!' I say, and rush to grab him, but William gets there first.

'Don't worry. He's a kind dog,' he says. 'Come and give him a pat.'

The girls come nearer to stroke him. Stan, of course, loves it and immediately lies down on the ground, legs in the air, head twisted on one side as they tickle his tummy.

'Where did he come from?' says Dora.

'Is he your dog, William?' says Nessie.

'No, he is Olivia's dog. The girl I'm going drawing with.'

For some reason this seems to offend Dora.

'I think you're being very rude!' she says. She stamps her feet and glares at him, ignoring me completely. 'If you don't want to go drawing with us then say so. *Anyway*, we aren't going drawing with you now, and I'm not going to let you play with my spinning top like I promised. I'm going to find Robert.' And she grabs the other little girl by her hand and they stomp off.

'What was all that about?' I say.

'I don't know,' says William, frowning. 'I'm sorry, Olivia. I will speak to her later.'

We cut across a field to a little walled garden, and suddenly I get a pang that Mum's not here to see it. Gardens are Mum's other passion, besides saving the world.

'It is really sweet. I wish I could show my mum,' I say.

'Your mother? I didn't realize she was here,' says William. 'I thought, as you only mentioned your father, that perhaps you had lost her.'

Lost her? That's a funny expression. I know where she is . . . Then I realize – he meant 'died'.

'I do have a mum but . . . she's . . .' The words stay as locked up as she is. 'She couldn't come.'

'I know!' said William. 'You wait here. I have my watercolours and brushes up at the castle, and plenty of paper. You can do a painting for her!'

'Thanks!' I say. 'Are you sure? That's so kind.'

'I won't be long,' says William. 'Take a seat and I'll run for my sketchbook. I will be back in a few minutes.'

I open the little gate and go inside the garden. The delicate flowers seem so fragile on this wild island, and the wall which shelters the plants from the sea winds creates a quiet place. A little refuge. It smells wonderful too, full of perfumes and sweet scents. I sit on the bench and look up at the castle. Stan lies down at my feet and I hear a lark sing. The sun is warm on my face, and I close my eyes for a minute. It is so peaceful.

And then I hear a gunshot. And screams.

Chapter Seventeen

The sounds come from the left. I run out of the garden as fast as I can, Stan at my heels. William is running down from the castle towards a boy about my age, who is on the ground. There's a lot of blood. Little Nessie is kneeling beside him, crying, her dress splashed with red. Dora is stood, screaming, holding a rifle, which she is pointing at the ground. William takes the rifle off her, breaks it across his knee and leaves it on the ground. He gets to the boy before me.

'I just wanted to hold it,' Dora says. She is standing there, shaking. 'I just wanted to hold it for a minute, but Robert wouldn't give it to me.'

'Get help!' William shouts at me and Nessie. 'I'll staunch the flow of blood.' I see him take off his jacket and then his shirt, leaving just some long-sleeved T-shirt on. He rips the shirt into strips, his actions quick and calm.

Nessie and I and Stan run together to the castle, but a tall man, also in costume, is already hurtling towards us.

'Professor! Dora shot Robert!' says Nessie, sobbing.

He charges past us down to William, who has tied the strips tightly around Robert's arm.

'Good lad, William,' I hear him say. 'Excellent work. Now, Robert, old man, you're going to be fine. I can see your sister has not done for you today. Be brave, old chap. I'm going to carry you to the castle.' He picks him up in his arms and they start off across the field, William and this professor carrying the boy between them, Nessie with her arms around the now-weeping Dora, following them.

I am not sure what to do. I am stood there staring, feeling sick.

I don't want to get in the way. They are managing without me. I'd better just go home.

'Come on, Stan,' I say, and he follows me.

Dad was in the kitchen when we got back.

'Olivia! That's a relief. I was getting worried about you!' he said.

'Did you hear the gunshot, then?' I said. 'I think the boy will be all right. They've taken him up to the castle.'

'What gunshot?' Dad said.

'A girl shot a boy by mistake. She tried to take his rifle off him – I think he was rabbiting or something – and it went off. But William – the boy I was with – stopped the bleeding, and then someone came down from the castle and they carried him up there.'

'How terrible!' Dad said. 'It must have been horrible for you, Olivia.'

I started shaking.

'Sit down. I'll make you something hot and sweet,' Dad said. 'I think you've got a bit of delayed shock.'

Dad guided me into the sitting room and tucked me up on the sofa with a duvet around me. He made some hot chocolate. My hands were trembling a bit, but he helped me take some sips, and sat down beside me. He hugged me close until my body calmed down. I felt really tired. I leant into him and felt his jumper against my cheek, and his dad warmth, and I started to feel better.

'I was thinking,' said Dad. 'How about if we go to Alnwick tomorrow? I want to pick up some

157

Edwardian magazines that Barter Books have put aside for me. We could make a day of it – visit the castle and the gardens. I'll keep my phone on and we'll keep checking up about your mum throughout the day. But only if you like. Obviously if you don't want to . . .'

I could tell he really wanted me to say 'yes'. It felt good to be wanted, but I knew I couldn't enjoy anything before getting news about how the boy was.

'That would be great, Dad,' I said. 'But would it be OK if I called up at the castle later to see how William and the boy who was shot are?'

'Of course. I'm surprised we haven't heard an air ambulance or something. Hopefully it is just a superficial wound.'

'William was very good at first aid. We learnt about stopping blood flow at cadets last week,' I said, without thinking.

'Cadets? Army cadets?' Dad said, sounding very surprised.

Oh no. I had blown my cover.

'Yes. Well, it's not cadets properly yet, but the school are setting up an army cadets division soon, and my friends and I have been having sort of taster sessions with our PE teacher. She's in the reserves.'

'A school division of army cadets? That can't have gone down well with your mum,' said Dad.

'Well . . .' I said.

Dad looked down at me. 'Does she know, Olivia?'

I sighed. 'She does.'

Dad still frowned. 'But wouldn't there have to be a form or something, for parental consent? I can't see her signing that!'

'There was. And she didn't,' I said. 'It was signed. Just . . . not by Mum.'

Dad sighed. 'I don't believe this. Why does my family not tell me anything? I think I can guess what happened. Your grandad signed it?'

I nodded.

'Is this what the newest big row was between your grandad and your mum? Your gran mentioned one, the last time she phoned.'

I nodded again.

'Your gran seemed to think it was your grandad's fault this time, not your mum's,' said Dad. 'She said it was just one of their usual arguments but you had got involved and were on your grandad's side, which was why you had decided to move back to the vicarage. When I asked more about it she wasn't keen to tell me – just said I wasn't to worry. She said it would all blow over and she would take your grandad away to get some distance, so you could move back to the flat for a bit and talk to your mum.'

So that was why they went on holiday so suddenly. I knew Gran wasn't happy about this argument.

'I shouldn't have let your gran keep me out of it,' Dad continued. 'I should have insisted she told me exactly what was going on. It was probably because your grandad and I had a row about cadets when I was a teenager, and she thought it might upset me again. But I *am* your dad, after all. She should have told me.'

His arms were still hugging me tight. It felt so good, so secure. The words spilled out of me.

'The thing is, Dad; Mum and Grandad aren't listening to each other. Mum is so angry about me joining the cadets. And you know Grandad, you know how much he loves the army. He said when he went to Afghanistan he knew he might not come back — he said the army even took a photo of him, and every other soldier, in case they got killed and pictures were needed for the newspapers. He knew he might die, but he still went, because he believed in it — in being a soldier. And Gran was so brave, waving him off, knowing he might be injured. Or worse. That he might not come back.'

'I know,' whispered Dad.

'Grandad was so pleased I wanted to join the cadets. I just think it will be fun,' I said. I was surprised to find I was crying. I wiped my arm angrily against my cheek and tried to stop my voice wobbling.

'And why do you think that?' said Dad.

I really liked the way Dad asked me – like he wanted to know more about my point of view, like he wouldn't be upset or disappointed about whatever I said. Not like when Grandad or Mum asked me things.

'I'm just good at the sort of things they do,' I said. 'Miss Potter says I'll love it because I'm sporty and calm and quick and practical, and I'll do really well. And I've been reading the cadet's handbook Grandad gave me. It's really interesting. You'd like it, Dad – there's even a link between the National Trust and cadets, because the woman who founded the National Trust was very keen on cadet groups, to help poor children learn things. And the things we will learn are so interesting – first aid and orienteering and climbing and camping. Even the marching – I didn't know before that drill is about getting soldiers quickly from one place to another. I know Mum won't understand, but we've had a go at it, and it's sort of satisfying getting it right. Like dance steps,' I said, turning to him.

'I can see that,' Dad said. 'I hated it myself. I found it all a bit much, being told what to do – it was so busy, and there didn't seem to be much time to think about things. I just felt rushed from one activity to another. I know your grandad was disappointed with me when I left. It wasn't so much that I was a pacifist, I just didn't enjoy those activities. I don't like guns, for a start. And I don't enjoy sporty things. But I can see how you might enjoy it.'

'The only thing is,' I said, and then took a deep, shaky breath. 'The thing is, since the school said we are going to have cadets, things have got nasty between everyone.' I had to stop for a moment. 'Really nasty. Some people don't want school cadets, and some others are angry that it might be cancelled, and now everyone in school is arguing about it. It's horrible.'

'Has anyone other than Mum said they don't agree with it?' Dad asked.

'Well, pretty much just Aidan Brocklesby and his family. They are Quakers. They don't want cadets based in the school.'

'Well, that's understandable, if they are Quakers,'

said Dad. He must have felt me stiffen, because he quickly gave me another hug and said, 'Look, Olivia, we don't have to talk about this if you don't want to. You've got enough going on. Let's cook some supper.'

Part of me was glad that Dad had changed the subject, but another part of me didn't really want to stop talking about it, now I had started. I knew eventually I was going to have to tell Dad exactly just how nasty it had got with Aidan. I wanted to; I needed to. I was glad I was miles away from home, on an island, but I knew it wouldn't be for ever. I would be going back to school in only a week, and I had to work out what to do before then. But I couldn't work this all out on my own. Things had got so bad I knew I had to voice an opinion. I couldn't just keep sitting on the fence, despite understanding where everyone was coming from. Eventually, I would have to say and do something.

I just had no idea what.

Chapter Eighteen

Dad cooked a creamy mushroom risotto for our evening meal, and then I baked some bananas and chocolate for him.

'Delicious!' he said. 'I didn't know you could cook, Olivia. Maybe you take after me in that way!'

It was really nice how pleased he was about that, even though I'd only put some bananas in an oven.

'I'll take Stan out, and see if I can find William,' I said. 'See how Robert is doing.'

'Great. I'll get on with some work, but let me know when you're back,' Dad said.

I headed out and walked straight to the castle. I couldn't see William there, and I couldn't even find how to get into the private apartments – it all looked shut up to me.

So I turn back and take Stan for a walk down through the village to St Cuthbert's Island, and there William is, sketching.

I cross over to the island. I like walking on the wet sand, glistening in the evening light, though it is a bit odd to think that it is normally covered in sea.

'Saint Cuthbert came here for peace and quiet,' says William, sitting on a rock.

The way he says it – pretend-cross but smiling – makes me laugh.

'It's not exactly hard to get to,' I say. 'Not when the tide is out like this. I saw people here this morning.'

'Did you?' says William. 'Well, I'm glad they are not here now.' But he looks over at me and smiles again, so I think he likes me being here. Which is good. I am happy to see him too.

'How is he, the boy who was shot?' I say.

'The wound is clean. They say he has a good chance of recovery,' he says.

'You were so good at dealing with it.'

William makes a face. 'Thank you. It wasn't pleasant. I learnt about it at our school cadets, of course, but I'd never actually seen the effects of a gunshot on a person before.'

'Me neither,' I say. I nearly ask him about his school cadets but he quickly changes the subject and, on second thoughts, it's fine with me not to think about it.

'Anyway, enough of that,' he says. 'The tide won't come in for a while. Would you like to sketch? Maybe do that picture for your mother? I have paper and paints.'

'Yes, I'd like to.' So we sit on the rocks and sketch the sea and the shoreline. There is a gentle breeze. The sea is ruffled but basically calm. Looking at the sea properly, I notice how it isn't quite the way I imagined it – the lines of waves aren't quite straight, the foam is more broken up. I like looking at things. Really looking. They aren't always what you imagine them to be.

William lets me use his paintbox. It is wooden and he has a little glass jar for the water. It's so old-school, I love it.

I sketch William. He laughs a little self-consciously when he notices. At first I feel a bit shy, but it is like when I was drawing Aidan – I concentrate on capturing William as he sketches, trying to capture his lines, the way he sits. William frowns a little, and then looks up and smiles at me, and for a minute he reminds me so much of Aidan when he was drawing me and I feel so, so sad. About everything. And it's too much to hold on to any more.

'My mother is a pacifist,' I blurt out. 'She's been arrested for causing damage in a demonstration.'

My eyes fill with hot, angry tears.

'Oh, Olivia, I'm sorry.' He passes me a handkerchief. It is white cloth, all neatly folded up. I've never met any boy like him. I wipe my eyes, and go to hand the hankie back but he gestures for me to keep it and I put it in my pocket.

'Thanks,' I say. 'It's just . . . I am so cross with her for doing that – for being arrested. We were going to spend time together and suddenly I'm sent miles away, so that I'm not on my own – that's why I am here with my dad.' I sigh. 'I'm cross about what she did because of that, but also, I don't even know if I agree that what she did was right. I am worried about what will happen to her, though. I know she is trying to do the right thing.'

William gives me a look of such understanding that I almost cry again. 'It is a really difficult subject. I've only just started thinking about it myself. Reading things. There are books in the library here – they are making me think in ways I have never done before. My father hates pacifists, and there is so much in the newspapers against them. One of my aunts even gives out white feathers to men who refuse to fight.'

'White feathers?' I say.

'Yes, white – you know, to symbolize cowardice.'

'I thought white symbolized peace, not cowardice,' I say. 'You know, like doves. That's why my mum gives out white poppies.'

'To be honest,' says William, 'I think it's because the white feathers are from chickens. And they are taken from . . . you know . . . not the best part of the hen.'

'Sorry, what do you mean?'

'I don't want to be coarse . . . The, er . . . the part where the eggs come from.' He's blushing a little.

Even though I am feeling so sad, a bit of me wants to laugh at this. He is such an odd boy!

'Anyway, I haven't heard of these poppies,' he continues, obviously not wanting to talk about hens or feathers any longer. 'What does she say when others ask her if she really wants us to do nothing to defend ourselves?'

'That's what Grandad says to her. But Mum says some politicians and newspapers deliberately get everyone all worked up about the need to defend ourselves from enemies and go to war, when the problems which actually exist could be solved by countries talking to each other instead. She says countries have diplomats to get people to listen to each other and come to agreements, and governments don't use them properly.

'She says the only people who benefit in wars are the people who sell the weapons, and we should think carefully about the fact that sometimes they are friends with the politicians and the newspaper owners who seem so keen on war. She says we shouldn't believe everything we see in all the papers, because sometimes the stories they tell us are not always completely honest. She says there is still propaganda, even in peacetime. And that in the end, all wars end with negotiation, so we should negotiate before, not after killing everyone, and for everyone's sake we have to find common ground.'

It felt good spelling out what Mum thought. It wasn't just nonsense. She made really good points.

'And your father? What does he think?'

'Well, he was a bit annoyed . . .'

'Annoyed!' William repeats, and laughs. 'That is surely an understatement. If my mother was arrested . . . What my father would think!'

'Dad says she is a good person. He is proud of her. Actually, I'm proud of her, William,' I say.

And suddenly I realize I am. I am actually more proud of Mum than embarrassed by her. She doesn't bully or say nasty things or try to stir things up between people, like Seb. I don't agree with everything she says or does, but at least she is trying to do what is right, like Aidan. And, like Aidan, she is suffering for it.

'I don't know if I agree with her about everything, but she's so brave,' I tell William. 'She believes in what she is doing. And she says we need to think more about the civilians caught up in wars. It's always the civilians who suffer most in war, she says.'

'Olivia, I don't want to upset you, but I am afraid that is not true,' said William. 'Perhaps your mother has been sheltered from the realities of warfare.'

'I don't think so,' I say. 'Mum has done lots of research.'

'But has she been to the front?' said William. 'My cousin was fighting there . . . I saw him when he was on leave. If you could have seen his eyes . . . He said it was like hell.'

I know Mum says civilians are now essentially on the front line in wars, because they get bombed and

170

shot at, but I take William's point. It must be even harder for the soldiers. 'Where is he now?'

'He is dead.'

I feel terrible. 'I'm so sorry, William.'

'That is why I must join the army when I turn eighteen next week. I've done my cadet training, and I know I am ready. When we sang "Jerusalem" today, it gave me strength. I feel that now I am completely recovered from my illness, God is telling me to give my life for my country.'

'I don't know, William. I don't understand why you'd have to be a soldier to do that. You could give your life in another way – you could be an artist for our country, or anything else really.'

'Do you really think so? You don't think that is being cowardly?' said William.

'Of course not!' I say. 'Isn't "giving your life for your country" a way of talking about using your gifts? You're really good at art.'

'That is true . . . There are war artists, like Muirhead Bone,' said William thoughtfully. He sighed. 'Well, it has been taken out of my hands, anyway. The government has said we must all join up,' he says. 'From eighteen to forty-one. Married or not.'

171

'That can't be right!' I say, shocked. 'When did that happen? Nobody said anything about that at school.'

'I am sorry, Olivia. I didn't mean to upset you, if your school or family hasn't told you. It is hard for the women. You must be brave. Your father, too, will go. I'm sorry.'

'No, you're wrong. I'm sure you're wrong, William.' I try not to panic. Dad? Fighting? That's ridiculous. How could they *make* my dad join the army? 'I'll ask Dad about this, and I'll prove to you that this is just a rumour. I don't know where you heard about it, but it's not true, I'm sure.'

William takes a round silver watch on a chain out of his pocket and looks at it.

'I am afraid I have to go very soon, Olivia, but thank you. Thank you for telling me about your mother. And talking about pacifism with me. And for your ideas about artists serving our country. I've been thinking and thinking about it all, but I hadn't yet spoken about these things with anyone else. I don't feel able to talk with my parents about it.'

'Just don't rush into things,' I say. 'The words in the hymn – in "Jerusalem" – did you know they are from a poem by William Blake? I don't think they mean what you might think they do. Mum always says they are about the mental fight – wars of ideas – not about fighting and going to war.'

'I would like to hear more of what you think,' William says. 'There's something about you. I feel I need to listen to you. Shall we meet tomorrow afternoon and sketch again? I cannot remember the tides – perhaps we should meet first in Miss Jekyll's garden and maybe go back down to the sea?'

'I'd like that,' I say.

I wait while William packs up his things, and we walk back to the shore. The sun is beginning to set, the clouds are so pretty and rosy. There are a couple of black and white oystercatchers still busy, their long red bills probing in the sand. The sea is coming closer. Soon the tide will be in.

Stan chases birds along the beach. They rise up in the air, crying indignantly, and he comes reluctantly to my call.

'Stop galumphing along!' I say to him.

'You know "Jabberwocky" too?' laughs William. 'My mother used to read it to me when I was a child.'

'So did mine,' I say.

I put Stan on his lead, and William and Stan and I walk back up the path to the road together.

'Olivia!' I heard Dad call. He was walking down the road towards us.

Stan barked and ran towards him.

'It's my dad,' I said, turning to William, to introduce him, but there was nothing but empty space beside me. He had already gone home.

Chapter Nineteen

'I was a bit worried about you,' Dad said, slightly embarrassed, as if he was worried I was going to be cross with him for making a fuss. 'It's going to be dark soon and you've been gone a while. I know you are upset about your mum and what might happen tomorrow so I just thought I'd come and check on you. I walked up to the castle to find the accommodation, but it all looked closed up. Hope that's OK?'

I liked that Dad was worried about me. That he came to check.

'It's fine. I was fine.' I smiled at him. 'I saw William nearby and we went drawing on St Cuthbert's Island,' I said, pointing back to it. I was surprised to see the tide was completely in and St Cuthbert's was cut off by the sea. It was good that we had left when we did. The sun was setting fast now.

'How old is William?' said Dad, as we walked back.

'He said he is going to be eighteen next week,' I said.

'Oh, he's older than I thought,' said Dad, looking a bit worried. I suddenly realized that William was a Year Thirteen. I didn't normally speak to Year Thirteens.

'I think I would like to meet him,' Dad said. 'You understand, don't you, Olivia?'

'Yes. But honestly, Dad, when you meet him you won't worry,' I said. 'He's absolutely not like any Year Thirteen I've ever met. He is much more . . . He just seems a lot younger.' I thought about him blushing about the white feathers and it made me want to giggle again. 'We're going to meet tomorrow afternoon and do some drawing in Gertrude Jekyll's garden – you can meet him then.'

'How was the boy who got shot?' said Dad.

'I think he's fine. The doctor told William he'll recover,' I said.

When we got back to the house, we put the TV on and watched a funny political panel show. Dad was impressed I got all the jokes.

'Well, living with Mum, I can't not know about

these sorts of things,' I said. It was true. Thanks to Mum, I knew more about politics than other people my age. Except maybe Aidan. It was a nice feeling, impressing Dad. Especially since I didn't show that side of myself much – particularly at school. With all that happened at home, I didn't need to be dealing with getting involved in those arguments at school too. Maybe one day, I thought, if people could just talk about these things without it turning into the big arguments it always seemed to at school, I wouldn't always have to keep that bit of me hidden all the time.

My stomach twisted. Mum. I just wanted them to let her go home.

'We'll know more tomorrow, Olivia,' said Dad, looking at me and squeezing my hand.

The next morning, I woke up at nine thirty. I'd slept late again. Maybe it was the sea air – that's the sort of thing Gran says. Or maybe it was that I just didn't want to wake and hear the news.

I went downstairs. Stan met me in the hallway, bowing and wagging his tail and rolling over for a tickle.

'You're a bit wet – and you smell seaweedy!'
I said. 'Dad must have taken you out already, but
you can come later when I go and see William.
You'd like that, wouldn't you?'

I knew I would, anyway. It was nice making
a new friend when stuff with the old ones was so
complicated.

Dad was on the phone, in the sitting room.

'No, I haven't seen the papers yet. They won't
be delivered to the island until later. I'll look online.
Wait a minute.'

Dad put his phone on the table and looked up
something on his laptop. He picked up the phone
again, smiled at me and mouthed, 'It's Johnny.'

My stomach lurched.

'OK, hold on a minute . . .' Dad said. 'No, no.
Can't see . . . Hang on a minute. Yes. Got it. Where
did they get that photo of her? She looks slightly
deranged.'

I looked over Dad's shoulder. There was a small
article on the demonstration. I was glad it was small
and clearly Dad had had to look hard to find it.
Hopefully Chloe and her family wouldn't have seen
it. There was a little row of pictures showing Mum
and the two other protesters who were arrested.

Mum's picture was of her in a long summer dress, holding a bunch of flowers.

I didn't think she looked deranged. She looked like a beautiful hippy. Her face was painted with flowers, she was smiling and her hair was long, with flowers in it too. I recognized it from the summer solstice celebration she organized last year in our local park. It didn't look particularly serious or political, but it didn't look dangerous either. I was glad, really. Next to her was a picture of an elderly, smiling nun – Sister Mary – and one of a man, someone called Bernard, who I had seen in our flat. I liked him, because he always washed up his teacup.

'Are they letting them come home?' I said.

Dad smiled reassuringly at me but spoke to Johnny.

'So, I'd imagine they won't be kept waiting much longer. And have you seen any coverage in any other papers?'

I could hear Johnny's voice murmuring at the other end, but not what he was saying.

'Hmm. Well, you would have expected some focus on the nun,' said Dad. 'The fact that she is so old and respectable will help. It's all good. OK, I will.'

Dad passed the phone to me and walked into the kitchen. Stan followed him hopefully.

'Hi, Olivia. OK?' said Johnny.

'How's Mum?' I said. 'Is she OK?'

Johnny sounded tired. 'She's fine. She's going up in front of the magistrate this morning. Hopefully she will get bail and get to go home. She's really sorry about messing you around like this, Olivia.'

'I'm OK here. Actually, I really like it. I mean, I don't like the idea of Mum in a cell, but I do understand. And it's good being with Dad. Tell Mum I'm OK. Give her loads of love. Tell her I'll see her soon. Maybe even tomorrow.'

But I suddenly didn't want to leave Lindisfarne quite that quickly. I liked the space, and I needed to think things through before I saw Mum again; decide what I thought about what she'd done. And Aidan . . . About where I was with the school argument – whether not taking sides *is* taking sides, and whether I like it or not.

Johnny sounded surprised and pleased. 'Thanks for being so great, Olivia,' he said. 'And I'll let you know as soon as they are released.'

'So, are you OK?' said Dad, coming back in as I hung up. 'I didn't mean to eavesdrop, but . . . I'm glad you like being here, Olivia. I'm really enjoying you being here.'

'I meant it, Dad,' I said. He looked really happy.

We went back into the kitchen. I put some bread in the toaster. Dad filled the kettle. We were quiet. Dad was easy to be quiet with. And then I remembered something I had forgotten to ask him about.

'That boy I met – William – was talking about the army,' I said, spreading butter on my toast and carrying it to the table. Stan lay down at my feet. 'But he thinks he doesn't have a choice – that he has to join, whether he wants to or not. He says the government is making everyone aged eighteen to forty-one join the army, and he thinks he will have to do it once he is eighteen. He says you will have to join up too. That's not true, is it?'

'No,' said Dad, and a strong sense of relief washed over me. 'How strange. Where on earth did he get that idea?' Dad put a hot mug of tea in front of me. 'Some politicians talk about bringing back compulsory national service – when men aged seventeen to twenty-one have to spend eighteen months in the army – but that ended in the early 1960s.'

'I told him it wasn't true.'

Dad nodded thoughtfully. 'There are always wild rumours going around, sensationalist headlines to get people to click on the online links, or buy certain newspapers. Tell him not to worry, though. I think I might tell him myself when I meet him.'

We left Stan with water and some little treats hidden in a rubber puzzle ball, and drove off the island to Alnwick, to collect Dad's box of books.

Barter Books was the most amazing bookshop I had ever been in. It was on the site of Alnwick's old Victorian railway station, and used the building – so there were high ceilings and skylights, and you could see where the waiting rooms were and everything. It even had a little model train whizzing around on the top of the shelves. It was really big, with sofas and open fires and places to eat and drink and bookcases everywhere, where there used to be railway tracks. You could spend days, months, years there and never read everything. It was full of people quietly browsing, looking through books alone or in couples, silently pointing out things they found, or heading to the till clutching something as if it was the most precious treasure they had ever held.

Dad's face was all lit up – you could definitely see he thought his box of old dusty books was the best treasure ever. The lady at the till explained that they had just bought it at an auction, and they had kept it aside for him to look through, as it contained books and magazines from the 1900s.

'This is wonderful!' he said, and bought the entire box.

I chose some novels to buy, and a DVD of *A Testament of Youth*, because I remembered Gran saying it was one of her favourite books and how she would love to see the film one day. Dad noticed me with it and suggested we could watch it together, that the book it was based on was very famous and set at the time of the First World War. Dad paid for my books and the DVD, so I decided I would use my own money to quickly buy something for Mum and Gran and Grandad. I figured I might be going home soon, and I might not get another chance.

The bookshop had some posters and postcards for sale. I picked some cards, thinking I might buy frames for them later.

It began to rain very heavily, so we stayed in the warm and had lunch at the bookshop. Dad was fidgety, looking longingly down at the box by his feet.

'Olivia, would you mind very much if we went back quite soon?' he said. 'I had wanted to take you to Alnwick Castle – it's where they filmed part of *Harry Potter*, and there are amazing gardens. I really want you to see it . . . but it's raining so hard, and –'

'It's all right, Dad,' I said, smiling. 'I think you should look in that box too. I'd like to see it all as well.'

'Would you?' said Dad, looking very relieved, and finishing his lunch quickly.

'I would. And I think Stan will be missing us,' I replied. 'We can go to Alnwick Castle and gardens another time. I'd like that. Maybe I'll come up here again this summer.'

Dad's phone rang.

'Hello, Johnny. What? Oh no,' he said.

I felt sick. Dad's face was suddenly so serious.

'What on earth will happen now?' he asked.

Chapter Twenty

'What's the matter?' I said as Dad tucked away his phone, notebook and pen, and looked at me.

'They have refused bail – they won't let them out, no matter how much money is promised.'

'But why?' I felt so shocked and angry. 'Mum isn't dangerous. I thought they only refused people bail when they think they might do something dangerous. Cutting a little hole in a fence isn't dangerous.'

'I know, Olivia, but unfortunately some people think questioning things is dangerous, and contradicting the government helps our enemies. To be fair, I don't think that's the issue here. They didn't just question, they actually damaged military property, and I think bail was refused because they wouldn't promise not to do it again.'

'What?' I said. 'Why not?'

Dad sighed. 'You know your mum. I think she didn't take kindly to being lectured by the magistrate. Apparently she and Sister Mary were asked to assure the magistrate that they would never damage military property again, and first Sister Mary said she couldn't in conscience promise that, if the government insisted on continuing to send weapons to oppressive regimes, and then your mum and the others agreed. I think, quite passionately, knowing your mum. Apparently the magistrate wasn't very impressed. So your mum and the others are going to be taken to prison until the hearing, which, luckily, is scheduled for next week.'

I felt so cross with them. Why did they have to make their lives so difficult? Why did they have to make their opinions known all the time? They had done their action. Why couldn't they have left it at that? Didn't Mum even want to come home? Hadn't she thought about me at all? I felt hurt and angry and a bit scared. I didn't agree with cutting holes in army fences, and I was really fed up with Mum for not promising she wouldn't do it again —but it made me feel scared to think that a magistrate could believe it would be worth keeping people in prison for. The punishment seemed too much for what they had actually done. Besides, couldn't the magistrate see what Mum and the others did wasn't really about the fence? What was dangerous about trying to make people think, to draw attention to what was going on? That's all Mum was trying to do. Maybe she shouldn't have damaged a fence, but she would say she wasn't hurting anyone. She wasn't the one dropping bombs.

The weather was truly awful as we drove back. The rain lashed down, so that no sooner had the windscreen wipers cleared the windows, raindrops covered the glass again. It made such a lot of noise that Dad and I didn't talk much. I think neither of us really wanted to. Dad told me not to worry, but you could tell he was. I couldn't see out of my windows, but looking ahead through the cleared arcs on the windscreen I could just make out the sign to Holy Island. I found myself leaning forward in my seat, as if that would help us get there more quickly. We got to Beal and then we were driving along the causeway – the rough, choppy sea on either side of us, some brave or foolish seabirds, dark shapes against the grey sky, being buffeted about up in the wind above us. I was glad we were staying in such a strong, secure house. The house welcome book said it had been a garrison for soldiers in the eighteenth century. I could imagine that. It felt like nature was at war with us and we needed to get to safety.

Stan was overjoyed to see us, and it was a great comfort to fling my arms around him.

'She's going to be in prison for a week,' I whispered to Stan. 'I'll spend the rest of half-term here. I'm sorry about Mum, but I'm still cross with her and I am quite glad about staying. I need the space, and I've got a lot to think about.'

Stan rolled over so I could tickle his tummy. Either he was completely heartless or he was saying, 'There's nothing you can do, just live in the moment.' Or he didn't really understand but wanted a tickle. Whatever the answer, it did help.

'Johnny has given us an address for your mum, and if we write something today then it should get to her by Friday,' Dad said, putting on the kettle. 'It's bad luck she got a particularly unsympathetic magistrate. I wish they hadn't asked them to promise not to do it again.'

'Why couldn't Mum have just promised never to do it again?' I said. 'She never thinks.'

'To be fair, I don't think that's entirely true,' said Dad. 'I'd imagine they felt that if they said what they did was wrong, they would be lying – they would be saying they shouldn't have done it, and they don't think that. They are facing the consequences of that now.'

'You mean, *we* are facing the consequences,' I said grumpily.

'Olivia, I hope that being on Lindisfarne with me isn't the equivalent of being in prison?' said Dad gently. I felt a bit ashamed. 'I said it was bad luck, because another magistrate might have handled it in a different way,' he said.

'Maybe that doesn't seem very fair,' I said, a bit grudgingly. 'It shouldn't depend on the individual magistrate how you get treated.'

'Many people in history have said that, Olivia,' said Dad.

'I'm still annoyed with Mum, though,' I said.

'Look,' Dad said. 'We both know your mum can be . . . stubborn. But she wasn't the only one. They all said they couldn't, in conscience, promise never to do something like that again. Did you really want her to remain silent and let the others take all the blame?'

I shook my head. This was making me feel uncomfortable. It made me think about not speaking up for Aidan, and leaving him to get all the blame.

But it wasn't the same. At least Mum agreed with the others. How was I supposed to speak up for Aidan, if I didn't even agree with him?

Dad saw me frowning. 'Look, Olivia, Johnny says your mum is really upset and a bit scared, and she feels really guilty about the impact this will have on you. I know she hasn't gone about things in the right way this holiday, and I was annoyed with her too at first, but I really think you have to try to forgive her. I think she could do with a little bit of love. I'm going to write to her and tell her not to worry and that we are having a lovely time. Do you think you could write something comforting too?'

I nodded. It was still raining and I knew William would not be out drawing as we'd planned, so I decided I'd better write to Mum instead. I was still cross with her, but at the same time I couldn't bear to think of her being so upset. Dad gave me a postcard of Lindisfarne Castle and a stamp. I made my writing big, so it wasn't so obvious I didn't have much to say. It seemed a bit mean to still be angry with her for what she had done, but I couldn't say I wasn't – even though, after talking to William and Dad about what Mum did and why, I realized I did understand more than I thought I did.

Dear Mum,

Don't worry about me — I'm fine. I hope they let you out soon. I've been thinking about why you do what you do. I still don't agree about the cadets, and I'm not sure about the demonstrations or damaging the fence, and I wish you could have just promised not to do it again, but I think I can see your point a bit more, and I'm really sorry you didn't get bail.

Love,

Olivia xx

I addressed it to the prison, using the address Dad gave me. It was so strange putting Mum's name above the prison address, and her having a prison number, like she wasn't a person any more. It made me feel horrible writing it. Nobody else's mum I knew was in prison.

Dad finished writing his letter and put a stamp on the envelope.

'I'll go and post them now, if you like,' I said. 'I don't want to miss the post.'

'I'm not sure if you haven't already,' said Dad.

'Well, I'd rather it be in the post box waiting,' I said. 'I'll take Stan for a walk too.'

'OK, but don't get too wet,' said Dad. 'When you

come back I'll make you hot chocolate and we'll open that box of books. Then maybe we can watch that DVD you bought tonight?'

Stan, as usual, was very keen to go out, and didn't mind the rain. I screwed up my eyes against it and bowed my head as I walked down to the post box, Stan trotting along beside me. I posted the card and letter.

I suddenly wished I had written a bit more. Been a bit kinder.

'Good luck, Mum,' I whispered. 'I love you.'

I feel warm sun on my cheek, and look up into a blue sky.

It is too blue. There are no rain clouds at all. I look down at the ground. It is dry.

Something very odd is happening.

'Stan, this isn't right, is it?' I say, but Stan just gives a deep woof and waves his tail.

It's only a short walk home but I feel like I can't get back quickly enough. Stan pulls me and we practically fly down the street. Only a few film extras are out, nobody else, and no one seems upset –

nobody is pointing up at the sky or looking puzzled. I can hear birds singing. We rush up the garden path and push open the side door.

'That was quick,' said Dad. 'I'm not surprised you cut the walk short. Thanks for doing that, Olivia. Come on, take off your wet coat and I'll make you that hot chocolate.'

'It's not raining any more,' I said.

Dad laughed. 'I think you'll find it is, Olivia!' He pointed to the window. A fresh gust of wind blew more rain against the pane. I could hear it, raining so hard. Raindrops covered the glass, and I could see that outside the sky was as grey as it had been all morning, the path as wet.

I shivered. Dad was right. My coat was wet. Stan's fur was wet, and the scent of wet dog filled the kitchen. It was pouring down outside. So why was I so sure I had seen that blue sky, and the dry ground beneath my feet?

'Are you all right, Olivia?' said Dad. 'You look very pale. Do you want to go upstairs and lie down for a bit?'

I nodded. I did feel strange.

Dad brought me up some hot chocolate and a buttered, toasted teacake, and then I fell asleep. When I woke up, I could smell something lovely. Dad was making a sort of stew, and when I went downstairs, the kitchen was full of comforting, herby smells. The rain still hurled itself against the window.

The box was open, and some yellowing papers and old books were spread out on the table.

'Sorry, I couldn't resist!' said Dad. 'You've had a good sleep – are you feeling up to having some dinner? Shall we get trays and bring it in to eat while watching that DVD you bought? We're a bit under siege from the weather.'

So we settled down in the sitting room and watched the film. It was about a girl whose brother and fiancé both went to fight in the First World War. In the end, she became a nurse and went to the war to help too. It was so, so sad to see – not only soldiers being killed and injured, but how much it hurt their friends and families. The film reminded me that there were real people it had happened to, and they were young, and they were on both sides, each with people who loved them. It must have been so terrible to live at that time.

'I'm glad we didn't live then, and you didn't

have to fight in the war, Dad,' I said, when the film ended.

'I'm glad too,' he replied.

We brought our trays back into the kitchen and I helped Dad load the dishwasher.

'So, would you like to see what else is in the box?' said Dad. I loved how keen he was to share his treasure chest with me. He pointed at the little yellowing newspapers, called *The Western Front*, priced two shillings.

'These are exciting to me because they were published by Edward Hudson, the man who owned Lindisfarne Castle.'

I picked them up. Every leaflet was full of drawings of the First World War, by someone called Muirhead Bone.

'So, did they send artists to the war?' I say.

'Yes, it was very important. Like war photographers now, they showed people the devastation of war, and it made people angry with the enemy and more keen to fight.'

'Didn't it make them want to become pacifists?' I say.

'Maybe for some it worked like that, but mainly the images in these types of publications were carefully chosen to work on people's emotions so they would support the war,' explained Dad. 'Images are always very powerful. You do get paintings being done at this time showing the horrors of the trenches, and there is the war poetry from people like Siegfred Sassoon and Wilfred Owen, who didn't glorify war, but, mainly, the difficulties of soldiers were underplayed to the public, and the emphasis was on the evil of the enemy, and going to war to protect civilians.'

It was all very interesting, but I suddenly couldn't take looking at these things any more. My head was too full of thoughts about wars; too much sadness, and no way of changing things. Though Vera Brittain – the nurse in the film – and people like Mum and Aidan and his parents didn't agree, and thought something could be done. They were so sure. Why wasn't I?

'I think I might go to bed,' I said. 'See you tomorrow, Dad. Thanks for dinner.'

'OK,' said Dad, already half lost in one of the pamphlets, but he put it down to give me a hug.

'I've had a lovely day with you, thank you,' I said. 'Even with everything about Mum.'

'Me too,' he said. 'And Olivia? I know it is worrying, but it will be all right. Sleep well.'

The thing is, I couldn't. The bed was warm and cosy and I felt really tired, but I just started thinking about school again and poor Mum and the other protesters in prison. What was it like in prison? What was going to happen at the hearing? What would people say? How would people at school react? I felt powerless. There was nothing I could do about anything – not about this, nor about what was happening at school with Aidan. But even if there was, would I ever be brave enough to do it?

Chapter Twenty-one

The day after everyone first got cross about Aidan's parents and their petition, we had art. We were supposed to be finishing our portraits. Aidan was really quiet. I wanted to say something, but I didn't know what. I knew I didn't have to justify not going on the demonstration with Mum, even if he had gone with his parents, but at the same time I wanted to tell him why I hadn't, and how hard it was living with Mum – to feel I had my own ideas, my own opinions. That it was so easy to get swept away, and I wanted time, and space, to work out what I really thought and felt about things.

Why did everyone expect people to take one side or the other? Why did people have to be so mean to people who don't agree with them? What was wrong with being quiet, thinking about things, understanding both sides?

Besides, Aidan didn't seem to want to talk to me. He didn't really look at me, apart from when he had to draw me. He wasn't looking at me to talk or to laugh – in fact, he didn't even make eye contact. I was just the sitter for a portrait, not a friend any more. And that made me feel sad. But it was too difficult to talk to him about it.

In PE there was no climbing wall, so I wasn't paired with Aidan then, at least. The sun was shining, so we did athletics. I chose some running. I ran around the track, grateful for the space to be alone. All the time I was running, I was thinking about what I was going to say to Mum when I got home. I was going to tell her she had to stop ruling my life, telling me what to do. It was up to me if I wanted to join the cadets, not her. She had to let me make up my own mind about things – she couldn't tell me what to think.

I was glad to have reached a decision, so I went over to the area where Riya was doing some javelin, and we had a bit of a chat.

'I'm really worried about what is happening with Aidan, Olivia,' she said, as we walked to collect our javelins. 'Did you hear Tyler and Harry making chicken noises at him in the corridor just now? I think Seb is getting people all worked up.'

'That's awful,' I said. 'I hate Seb. He just enjoys fights and making trouble. But what can we do?'

'We can make it clear Aidan isn't alone in his beliefs, and then Seb will back off. He doesn't enjoy fights if he thinks he won't win. He's just a bully. We have to make it clear where we stand.'

I sighed. Why did it always have to come back to that?

Riya looked at me. 'Well, doesn't your mum mind about cadets too? I'd have thought she would.'

Why do people always think that what my mum thinks, or my grandad thinks, is what I think?

'Yes, she does. It's all a bit tricky,' I said.

'In what way?' Riya asked.

'Well, you know the permission slip and stuff? I didn't exactly tell her we were going to have cadets at school.'

'Olivia! She didn't know? Your mum will go mad. Look at how she was with the poppies!' said Riya.

'She already found out from the website. She is really angry.'

'So why did Mrs Opie say you were joining the cadets, then?' said Riya. 'Your mum will never give you permission.'

'I got Grandad to sign the slip. She found out about that too.'

'Olivia! Good luck tonight, then,' said Riya, shaking her head.

Nothing more was said about things until we walked back to the lockers at hometime. We heard shouting, but there was a group of people blocking the corridor.

'What's happening?' said Riya to Chloe and Nola, who were standing on the outside of the crowd.

'Aidan and Seb are fighting!' Nola said.

We pushed our way through. It was odd because there were loads of white feathers on the floor for some reason, like a pillow had burst, but Aidan and Seb weren't having a pillow fight – they were really hitting each other hard, and it seemed like Aidan was winning. Seb's face was red and he was panting. Aidan looked much fitter, but angry in a way I had never seen him be before. It was scary. This was gentle, funny Aidan. Something was badly wrong, if he was fighting.

'Hey!' shouted Miss Gavin, coming out of a classroom. 'What's going on here? Stop that, at once!'

They broke apart, though I noticed Seb tried to sneakily land another blow on Aidan while Miss Gavin pushed her way through the bystanders.

'What's all this mess? What do you think you are doing?'

'They are fighting, miss,' said Zoe, sounding a bit too excited.

'I can see that,' said Miss Gavin a bit unreasonably. 'Who started the fight?'

'Aidan did, miss,' said Tyler. 'He opened his locker, a load of feathers fell out, and then he turned and hit Seb.'

'Is this true?' said Miss Gavin to Aidan.

Aidan nodded. He wiped his nose – it was bleeding. I wished I had a tissue to give him. I wished I could get him right away from school, to be honest. Everything had become really nasty. He looked really miserable now, rather than furious. I felt so sorry for him.

'I didn't do anything, miss,' said Seb. His nose was bleeding too.

'That's not true, miss,' said Abhishek. 'Seb's been calling Aidan's parents cowards, miss. He's been getting at him all day – making chicken sounds at him in the corridors, and in football he kept fouling him and saying things.'

'And what's all this with the feathers?' said Miss Gavin. 'No, don't bother telling me. I'm sick of you both. I don't know what is going on, but violence is never a way to resolve disputes. I am surprised at you of all people, Aidan Brocklesby. You can both come with me to see Mrs Opie.'

And she marched them off, only turning back to look at Tyler and Abhishek.

'And you two, you can find a broom and sweep up this mess.'

Most people drifted away, including Tyler, but Riya and Chloe and Nola and I stayed with Gareth and Abhishek. White feathers were everywhere.

'I'll go and get a dustpan and brush,' said Chloe, and went off to the caretaker's office.

'I don't understand about the feathers,' said Abhishek, looking at them.

'It's not fair, Tyler leaving Abhishek to clear everything up,' said Gareth. 'It was Seb's cousin who put the feathers in his locker. She pretended she couldn't get into her locker so she could get a skeleton key from the caretaker. I heard her tell Chloe. She was standing in the corridor when Aidan opened it, with a big grin on her face, but she disappeared as soon as Miss Gavin came along.'

We turned and looked at Chloe, who was coming back down the corridor.

'Is it true that Seb's cousin put the feathers in Aidan's locker?' said Nola.

Chloe looked uncomfortable. 'Well, yes. I think it was just a joke,' she said.

'It's a bit of an odd joke,' said Gareth. He bent down and picked up a piece of paper lying on the floor.

Coward and son of cowards, it said.

'Aidan was reading a bit of paper before he turned around and hit Seb,' said Gareth. 'Maybe this was it.'

'So, did Seb's cousin put that there too?' I asked.

'I don't know,' said Chloe, but I didn't quite believe her.

'I've never seen Aidan hit anyone, ever,' said Abhishek.

'It was a good punch,' said Gareth.

'He must have been really upset,' said Nola. 'And I think it was really mean of Miss Gavin to say she was surprised at him. Like it was worse him hitting Seb than Seb hitting him.'

'Well, it was really,' said Chloe. 'I mean, Seb didn't hit him first, and he is supposed be a Quaker and not want to fight and everything. And his parents are doing that horrible online petition and trying to bully us into not having cadets. So he's just as bad as them.'

'That doesn't make any sense, Chloe,' said Riya.

'Stop talking to me like that,' yelled Chloe. 'Stop patronizing me. All I know is that Aidan Brocklesby is a big hypocrite. He starts fights and he can't take a joke.'

'Some joke!' said Riya. 'That note is horrible.'

'I don't know anything about the note,' said Chloe. 'As far as I'm concerned, it was just about some feathers in a locker, and Seb and his cousin were only having a bit of fun. Aidan Brocklesby is too up himself. I thought he was really vicious, the way he hit Seb. Seb's nose was bleeding.'

'So was Aidan's,' I said. I felt really angry.

'Well, I think you should be angrier with Aidan, Olivia. I think it's horrible what his parents are saying about your grandad and you, having a petition against cadets and everything. And Nola, your brother was even killed in combat. Do you think it's OK them saying bad things about the army?'

'You're just talking rubbish!' said Riya. 'Having a petition against school cadets is not the same as attacking the army! Stop making this so personal!'

'Well, you're only being horrible to *me*,' said

Chloe. She was really red and looked as if she was going to cry. What Riya was saying made more sense, but I hated seeing Chloe look so upset. I didn't know what to do.

'I'm going,' Chloe said, a moment later. And she walked off.

'I'd better go with her and see if she's OK,' said Nola, and ran off after her.

'Thanks for helping,' said Abhishek to us, and he and Gareth went off with the dustpan and brush.

Riya picked up a stray white feather.

'I've got a feeling this means more than we know,' she said.

And now, thanks to William explaining about white feathers, I knew she was right.

I really hated the fight. It wasn't funny or exciting, like some of the others thought. I think the scariest thing for me was seeing, right in front of me, how people could really want to hurt each other – and even Aidan could be pushed into doing that. I'd never seen Aidan so angry. He was always so calm, so good natured, so kind, but I saw him punching Seb as hard as he could. I'm not saying he didn't have every right to be angry, but it just shocked me how good he was at fighting. He was winning. I'd never thought of Aidan wanting to hurt anyone before – I'd never thought of him actually hurting someone – and I found I didn't like it. It wasn't Aidan. It had made me feel horrible that things had got so bad at school that even Aidan wanted to fight.

And when I got home that evening, it had been horrible too.

'I can't believe you went behind my back like that!' Mum said. 'And I think it's totally out of order of the school to do this. I want your education to help you ask questions, and making army cadets part of school life makes it impossible for you to stand outside it and ask if military action is good in the first place. Education is supposed to help you make your own decisions.'

I couldn't take this any more. 'How is it different to you and home? You making pacifism part of our home life makes it impossible for me to properly decide for myself if pacifism is good,' I shouted. 'And nobody is *making* anyone join the cadets.'

Mum, of course, ignored any alternative view. My alternative view. 'But how will it be at school for people like Aidan, if he doesn't want to join? How would your friends react if *you* didn't want to, Olivia? In this town, of course the children want to join the cadets. This town loves the army. Most of the families have relatives in it. It's peer pressure. I worry that if someone like Aidan doesn't join the cadets, it will be very obvious and he will be a social outcast. And I really don't think the army should have a presence in schools. I totally support the online petition the Brocklesbys have started. I'm going to tell your Head that I object to her using your photo for her own agenda, and that I withdraw permission for you to attend cadets.'

'You can't do that!' I said.

'I can,' said Mum. 'I'm sorry, Olivia, but you are *not* joining the cadets.'

'Yes, I *am* joining the cadets,' I said. 'And if you won't let me do it when I live with you, then I will leave home and go and live with Grandad.'

Remembering school and that argument at home, on top of worrying about and being cross with Mum in prison, was making me feel so miserable that I couldn't sleep. I took down a book from the bookshelves and tried to read a bit, and it helped. It was *Alice Through the Looking Glass*, so I found 'Jabberwocky' and remembered William instead. At least he was still friends with me. I thought about the sea and the seabirds and drawing William, and I drifted off to sleep at last.

It was Stan who woke me up. He was downstairs, woofing. My phone said it was three in the morning. I waited to hear if Dad's door opened, but it didn't. Gran always says Dad sleeps through everything.

So I went down. Stan was really agitated, pawing at the door to go out.

'Stan, I can't go out. Look – I'm in my pyjamas,' I said. 'Go back to your basket.' But Stan kept jumping up at the door.

'OK, OK.' I opened the door. 'You can do a wee in the garden,' I said, but Stan was off down the path before I could stop him. I looked up and saw that the gate had been left open, and he charged out on to the street.

'Stan! Come back!' I yelled, and grabbed Dad's raincoat and Stan's lead and the house keys hanging on the hook, put on my wellies and ran out into the dark and the rain.

I saw Stan rush down to the main street, and then turn left, towards the castle. I ran after him and eventually he stopped.

'Stan, come here! Good boy! Come here!' I called.

He ran back to me, his tail wagging, and woofed, but before I could grab him, he turned and ran away again, down towards the sea, and was swallowed up into darkness.

It was so quiet and dark – so dark – and cold and rainy. What was he doing? There weren't any street lights. I wished I'd brought a torch. I could hardly see where I was going as I ran down the street. I could hear the sea, and feel the cold rain on my face, and I seemed to be running into a wall of darkness.

'Stan!' I shouted.

And then I come out into the light.

Chapter Twenty-two

The sky is blue, and the sun is shining and it is warm. Really warm. I have to take Dad's coat off and put it over my arm. Even my pyjamas seem too thick for the weather.

So, this is a dream, I think.

I can see William walking up the road to the castle, away from me, his art bag over his shoulder. Stan gets to him first, and I see William pat him and then look back and around for me.

'Olivia!' William says, smiling. 'You look very artistic!'

I will have to tell William about this dream and the funny things he said.

'I've been trying to paint the sea, but now I thought I'd go back to the castle,' he continues. 'Would you like to join me?'

'OK,' I say.

He gives me a peppermint and I suck it. It's a really good dream, because I can taste its minty sweetness.

'This island is so beautiful,' he says, as we walk up. 'It is thought-provoking to consider its past – the vikings, the monks. It's wonderful to think they saw the same seabirds, the same light on the water, that we do.'

'I keep meaning to visit the priory,' I say.

'They say there are ghosts there,' says William.

'Do you believe in ghosts, then?' I say.

'I'm not sure,' says William. 'I know many do.'

We get to the castle, and when we arrive the man who had helped when the boy got shot comes out and smiles. He is wearing the same clothes as before. I'm the only one in pyjamas. Thanks a lot, dream.

'Ah, William! I believe there is post for you.'

'Thank you, Professor Lodge,' said William. He turns to me. 'I wrote to my sister after our conversation about pacifism,' he says.

'Pardon?' says the professor. 'I don't recall such a conversation.'

'I'm sorry, sir. I was talking to my friend Olivia here. I have brought her to the castle to meet you.

Professor Lodge, this is Miss Olivia . . . I'm sorry, I don't know your full name, Olivia.'

But before I can say anything, the professor speaks again. 'Who are you talking to, William?' says Professor Lodge. He is frowning.

William points at me. 'Olivia, of course.'

'But William,' says Professor Lodge, 'there is no one there.'

'Excuse me!' I say.

Even in the dream, I feel indignant. I might be in pyjamas, but I am there. It's my dream after all.

'But sir, Olivia is right here, beside me,' says William.

'I am sorry, my boy,' the professor says, 'but there is nobody with us.'

'You *are* here, aren't you?' says William to me, his hand reaching out to mine. His hand is hot. He is as real as I am, in this dream.

'Yes, of course I am,' I say. 'I don't know what is happening.'

'Come inside, William. You have been ill. I will ask the girls to get Mrs Lutyens,' says the professor. 'Nessie! Dora!' The two little girls we met before come running. 'Go and get Mrs Lutyens immediately! Bring her here.'

Professor Lodge puts his arm around William's shoulders and leads him inside. Stan and I follow.

'Is William ill?' I say, but the professor ignores me.

'Perhaps the dog should stay outside, William,' he says.

'I don't want to leave Stan,' I say.

'Olivia doesn't want to leave him,' says William.

'Olivia doesn't want to leave him?' says the professor, as we walk inside. 'Then of course he must come in.' But he still hasn't said a word directly to me.

'What's going on, William?' I say.

'I don't know,' says William. 'I don't understand.'

'Shhh, my boy, don't worry,' says the professor.

We go inside the castle. The wind indicator is the same, maybe a little brighter in colour, but everything else inside the castle in the dream is different from real life, in a very important way. The information desk and the place where I bought postcards have gone from the hallway, and there is a smell of some rich stew. To my left, I can hear the clattering of saucepans and see someone cooking in the kitchen. Somewhere in the distance, I can hear a cello play. This is a place where people are living, not just visiting.

There is the sound of running feet, and Nessie and Dora come back, followed by a woman in a long skirt and frilly blouse, her hair up, the way the extras wore it in the church.

'William, come and sit down. The girls say you are unwell,' she says.

'Thank you, but I am not. I have just bought my friend Olivia to meet you all,' says William. We are led into the dining room. The table is already set for a meal.

'Oh, *Olivia*!' says Dora, scornfully. 'He is always pretending to talk to some girl who isn't there.'

'That's rude!' I say.

'Shh,' Professor Lodge says. 'I believe he speaks the truth.'

'You mean . . .?' says the lady.

'I do,' says the professor. 'It is extraordinary. None of the conditions we normally see for communing with spirits seem to be present, but he appears to be communing with a spirit called Olivia.'

'What's he talking about?' I say.

'The dog, I think, is important,' Professor Lodge continues. 'Perhaps it is some sort of medium. He says it is accompanying the spirit.'

'What do you mean? I am not some spirit!' I say.

The dream is getting frightening. I try to pinch myself to wake myself up.

'Ow!' I say.

Nobody else reacts except William, who looks at me.

'Ask her to move one of these glasses,' says Professor Lodge.

I pick one up and move it.

They gasp.

The girls scream.

I can't see what they are making such a fuss about.

'Go to your rooms, my dears, but there is nothing to be frightened of,' says the woman.

The girls run off.

'What's going on?' I say to William. 'I don't like this.'

'I don't know,' he says. 'I don't understand.' He is sitting at the table looking bewilderedly from me to Professor Lodge, to Mrs Lutyens.

'It's quite simple,' says Professor Lodge. 'It is clear that this Olivia is a spirit from beyond the grave, who has come through the ether to talk to you.'

'You're not, are you? You're not from beyond the grave?' says William to me.

'Of course not!' I say, rubbing my hand from the

pinch. 'I don't know what this ether is either. I'm as alive as you are. I ate your peppermint just now. I sat beside you and painted. What are they going on about?'

'She is as alive as we are,' William tells the others. 'She eats and drinks and paints like us.'

'She eats and drinks, you say?' says Professor Lodge eagerly. 'What sort of things?'

'I don't know,' I say. 'Sunday lunch, mints, ice cream. The usual things. What does he want to know?'

The professor still looks at William, waiting for an answer. Either he genuinely hasn't heard me or he is very rude.

'Um. She says she eats the normal things,' says William. 'Sunday lunch, peppermints, ice cream.'

'The normal things!' The professor seems to be nearly crying. 'I knew it was true,' he says, and now he is smiling but his eyes are full of tears. 'Raymond is eating what he loves, he is drinking what he loves . . . My boy is smoking cigars, drinking whisky.' Then he gets out a handkerchief and blows his nose, before going on. 'And tell me, are there trees? Are there houses and flowers in her world, as in ours?'

'Of course there are!' I say. I don't like this joke.

'She says, "Of course there are",' says William.

'And . . . has she met Raymond? May I ask her that? Could you ask her that?'

'Have you met Raymond?' says William, in a puzzled way.

'Raymond? No. It sounds like he is dead — isn't he?' I ask.

'Yes, in 1915. Last year,' says William.

I feel a bit sick. Dreams are strange, but this doesn't feel right at all. 'But . . . it isn't 1916 now,' I say.

'Yes it is,' says William. 'It is July 1916.'

'What is she saying?' says Professor Lodge. 'Could I speak to my boy?'

It is all too weird. These people asking me questions, but not being able to see me. Talking to the dead. William saying it is 1916.

If this is a dream, it is turning into a nightmare. Why can't I wake up?

'I've got to go,' I say. 'William, this is freaking me out. I will see you later. Come on, Stan.' I start to back away.

'She hasn't met Raymond and she has to go,' I hear William say. 'But she will come back.'

'Excellent,' says the woman. 'We will make sure we are ready.'

I grab my coat and I run. Even in the dream, I notice how my wellies feel awkward on the cobbled stones. I can see Stan on the lead, running beside me, down from the castle on to the road.

'Wake up! Wake up!' I keep saying to myself, pinching myself until I want to cry.

How can I be stuck in a dream I can't wake up from? We get to the harbour and then Stan, running before me on the lead, suddenly disappears right in front of my eyes.

'Stan!' I call, feeling him pull me forward with him, and then it all goes black.

Chapter Twenty-three

I was standing on the road in the dark, and it was raining. Stan was beside me, panting. I started shaking. This was not the way a dream ends. A dream ends with you waking up warm in bed – not cold and wet and shivering on a road.

I started to cry, and ran home as fast as I could, my hand shaking as I fumbled for my keys and opened the door.

'Dad! Dad!' I called as soon as we were inside. 'Dad! Dad! Help me!'

I heard Dad's bedroom door open and he rushed downstairs in his pyjamas, his hair standing up on end.

'Olivia!' he said. 'What's the matter?'

'I don't know. I don't know what is happening. I was in bed. I thought I was dreaming. Then I found myself on the road. With Stan. In the dark.'

Dad hugged me close.

'Sleepwalking. I used to do it whenever I was stressed. It's all the worry about your mum, I'm sure. Take off your wet things and change. Go back to bed and get warm.'

I changed into a dry T-shirt and leggings, and got back into bed. I couldn't stop shaking. Dad brought me up a cup of hot milk.

'You've been through a lot in a few days,' he said. 'Maybe you need a morning in bed. A proper rest.'

I nodded. That sounded good. I felt so mixed up, I didn't know what was going on any more. I drank the milk and put my head on the pillow and fell asleep.

Dad woke me up, knocking on the door.

'Come in!' I said, opening my eyes. The sleepwalking dream was still as clear as if it had really happened. It hadn't slipped away, like most dreams do. I wished it had.

Dad sat on my bed with a tray. He had made me a boiled egg and soldiers and a mug of tea with *Keep Calm and Carry On* on it. He had a mug too, which said *Shop Till You Drop* on it. Not really appropriate for Dad. Unless he's in Barter Books.

I dipped the soldier in the egg.

'Do you want to get up, or have some more sleep?' said Dad.

'I think I'll get up,' I said. I didn't want to be alone with my thoughts. I didn't want to think about my dream. Or fall asleep and have it again.

I wanted, most of all, to go and look for William. I needed to see him in reality, to get the sleepwalking dream out of my system. I thought I might even tell him about it, though it might be a bit embarrassing to tell him I was dreaming about him, when I hardly know him.

I wondered why I was dreaming about him, rather than Mum or Aidan. Perhaps it was my brain giving me a rest. Maybe, deep down, I didn't want to dream about anything to do with home when it was in my head every second I was awake.

I watched Dad as he left my room. I knew he meant it when he said I could talk to him about anything, but he looked worried enough already – and now he had a sleepwalking daughter, on top of everything else. So I thought I'd better keep all the horrible school stuff to myself.

After the fight and feathers at school, and the argument with Mum at home in the flat, things got worse very quickly. I ran upstairs and packed my overnight stuff in a bag and marched to the front door.

'I'm going back to live at the vicarage – I'm going to Gran and Grandad's,' I shouted back over my shoulder.

'Fine!' said Mum.

'And I'm not coming back!' I said, as I slammed the door behind me.

Gran was surprised, but pleased to see me when I rang the vicarage door an hour later.

'Hello, Olivia love,' she said, giving me her usual hug. 'It's lovely to see you, of course, but why are you here tonight?'

'Can I move back in with you, Gran?' I said. 'I just don't fit in at home with Mum any more. I want to join the cadets at school and she won't let me. All her friends are always over and I can't get my homework done.'

I knew that would be important for Gran. She was always worrying about my homework.

'Is that Olivia I hear?' said Grandad, coming down the hall.

'Come in, Olivia,' said Gran. 'Andrew, Olivia wants to come and stay with us.'

'Mum won't let me join the cadets and I'm just fed up with people always being in the flat, organizing demonstrations,' I said. I was exaggerating, but I knew it annoyed Grandad too.

I suppose I was being a bit manipulative, but I knew I had to move out if I was going to have a normal social life. I couldn't imagine ever making new friends and bringing them back to my home. I couldn't cope with watching their faces as they stepped inside Mum's flat, trying to second-guess their reactions as she chatted to them. She was too friendly, too interested, too open. And I know those qualities are supposed to be good, but it isn't easy if your mum just won't keep her opinions to herself. I didn't have the energy to explain, every time someone visited, that even if I lived in a home covered with political posters and cards and slogans, which had activists in and out all day, I didn't necessarily agree with everything on the wall or everyone there. I lived there, but my point of view wasn't reflected in our home. Not that I was always all that sure what my point of view was, to be honest. All I knew was that if I stayed with Mum, all the arguments I had with her would only get worse – she would never, ever see any other way of looking at the world. I had to be my own person. All I had left was walking out. If she wouldn't listen to my words, I had to show her, by my actions, that I didn't agree with her.

Gran turned to him. 'I'm not sure, Andrew. We don't want to fall out with Caz.'

Grandad harrumphed a bit. 'I don't see that Caz has worried much about how her actions impact on us, or, indeed, Olivia.'

'Andrew!' said Gran.

'Please, Gran. I just can't work at home,' I say. 'I'm falling behind at school.' Which was actually a lie. 'And Mum said it was fine if I moved back with you.' Which was horribly true.

'So, what are you asking, Olivia?' asked Gran worriedly.

'I want to live with you both, not Mum,' I said.

'Look, come and stay this week, and I will talk to your mother,' said Grandad.

'I wonder if I should speak to her, rather than you, Andrew,' said Gran. 'You know how you and Caz –'

But the phone rang, and Grandad had already picked it up.

'The vicarage. Ah, yes, Caz. Yes, she is here. Yes, yes, I did give my permission for her to join the cadets ... What do you mean? No, *you* are trying to brainwash her, not me. Pardon? As far as I'm concerned, she can stay here as long as she likes. I will let Olivia decide, not you ... Because I respect her! She is a very mature young woman, which is more than I can say for her mother,' he said, and put down the phone. 'Unbearable!' he added, to no one in particular, and marched into his study, closing the door.

Gran looked at me and made a face. 'We'd better let him cool off, Olivia. You know how he and your mum get. They love each other, but they do rub each other up the wrong way. I think perhaps you had better ring her later.'

'Do I have to?' I said.

Gran nodded. 'You can stay for a few days until this all blows over, but then you have to go home.'

The trouble was, it didn't blow over. Mum said I could stay with Gran and Grandad for as long as I liked, but it was a tricky, 'I-respect-your-decision-but-I-don't-agree-with-you' and 'I-am-very-hurt-but-I-am-giving-you-space-because-I-have-read-all-the-right-parenting-books' type of conversation. Not that she mentioned the parenting books, but I had seen them on her bedside table. She didn't only read books about politics. I knew she was upset and doing her best, but she also seemed to genuinely believe she wasn't putting any pressure on me, and that really irritated me.

So I ended up living back at Gran and Grandad's indefinitely, which was what I wanted. But it didn't feel as good as I wanted it to. It wasn't nice knowing Mum was so cross and hurt with me about going behind her back. I had never done that before, and even though I still felt she hadn't given me much choice, it just made me feel a bit sad and cross too. And I still didn't know if I would actually be able to do cadets. Since it wasn't starting until the new school year, I thought it best to let it be for now.

Gran wasn't as happy as usual about me being there. I kept catching her sighing or looking worriedly at me. And it was true that there was more room at the vicarage and it was nice to be back in my big room, but both of them seemed to be really busy, more busy than they were when I'd stayed before.

I felt a bit lonely, but when I asked if I could invite Nola back during the week or at the weekend

Gran said, 'Not this week, Olivia, it's a bit difficult,' which she never normally said.

So I got a lot of work done over that week because there was nothing much else to do. I did go to town at the weekend and met Chloe and Nola out shopping. Riya didn't want to come because she and Chloe weren't speaking to each other much after the row about Aidan. Our friendship group was breaking up, and it was horrible. I had to be more careful than ever not to cause our last bit of group to fracture apart.

'So, are you living with your gran and grandad for ever, then?' said Chloe.

'I want to,' I say. 'I'm fed up with Mum.'

'Isn't she upset though, your mum?' said Nola. 'I mean, she really loves you, Olivia.'

I shrugged. 'Funny way of showing it then,' I say. 'Not letting me join the cadets when it's something I really want to do.'

'She said you couldn't?' said Chloe. 'That's awful!'

Chloe made me feel a bit better about it.

I did think about texting Mum from time to time, but I wasn't sure what to say. Besides, she wasn't ringing or texting me either.

It was a bit miserable at school too. Nothing

much was happening in classes. We had a different still-life project and I wasn't teamed up with Aidan any more for art, and I missed that. And anyway, he'd been off school since the fight. There were rumours going round that he was suspended, though I thought it wouldn't be fair if he was, because Seb was still at school. So I was with Chloe for climbing, and she wasn't as good as Aidan and kept laughing when she made a mistake, which made me nervous. With Aidan, I could concentrate on climbing and just absolutely trust he would keep me safe. I couldn't trust Chloe that way. I missed him. We didn't even have any more cadets' taster sessions with Miss Potter – Seb said it was because of the petition and Mrs Opie wanting to not have an argument and get Aidan's parents cross.

'So, the Quaker bullies are winning, then,' said Chloe. 'That's terrible!'

'How does a petition bully anyone?' said Riya, overhearing her. 'Saying you disagree with something isn't bullying. It's a human right.'

'It's my human right not to be blown up by terrorists,' said Chloe.

Riya rolled her eyes. 'The petition has nothing to do with terrorists. It's Aidan's parents organizing it, for goodness' sake. For the millionth time, this is just about whether or not cadets should be in school.'

'Eddie was a cadet,' said Nola. 'It's not like cadets are a bad thing.'

'I know,' said Riya. 'But maybe . . . maybe he was good at sports and went to cadets and then just automatically went on to the army and then to fight in Afghanistan, without really thinking about how he might have to kill and even be killed. Maybe being in the cadets made it a natural choice for him to be a soldier, and he didn't properly think of the alternatives. Maybe he was too young when he signed up. Maybe he should have just been able to do sport, stay at school and not think about the army at all until he was older. And if we have cadets in school, as part of our everyday routine, maybe it will be even harder to not think the army is a natural thing to do with our lives.'

She said it gently, and you could tell she didn't want to hurt Nola. But she said it anyway. I remembered Nola and Eddie's uncle and aunt crying in the pub after the funeral. Even if she wasn't right – even if Eddie had gone off to the war knowing exactly what he was doing and knowing he was going to kill and maybe be killed – she was still brave to say what she said. Because these were important points and I hadn't heard anyone else say that out loud.

Nola lifted her chin and stared at Riya. 'It *was* a natural choice for Eddie. He wanted to be in the army. He loved it.'

'That's good, then,' said Riya. 'I'm glad to hear it.'

'So, have you become one of them too, then?' said Chloe. 'Are you a pacifist like Aidan?'

'I don't know,' said Riya. 'But the way some people are treating him and talking about the petition makes me worried. If people can get so angry just because someone politely asks for something not to happen, then I don't know if the thing at the centre of it all is a good thing to happen. I'm glad Mrs Opie isn't rushing into things. Aidan's getting horrible hate messages online and someone even sent hate mail to his parents and painted graffiti on their house. I don't like that. Nobody should.' Riya put her bag on to her shoulder and went to the library. She spent a lot of time there now.

I should have said something. I should have gone after Riya and asked her about Aidan and the hate messages. I should have told her how brave she was, saying these things. I should have been like her. And I should have challenged Chloe and Seb more, got involved and pointed out that they were acting like bullies and making a bad atmosphere. But at that time, I still really wanted cadets at school, and I was cross with Mum. So I just kept my head down.

Then Thursday happened. The day the *Gazette* came out. With a letter from Mum in it.

I only found out about it in the evening.

Grandad was really angry.

'Caz really doesn't know what she is talking about!' he said to Gran, coming into the kitchen and waving the paper in front of her, as she was trying to make dinner.

'Andrew – shh,' she said, looking over at me. I was in the kitchen too, as I had offered to peel the potatoes. I felt like I wanted to do something to make Gran pleased with me, instead of worrying her. I felt that Mum had somehow made her feel guilty for me coming to live with her and Grandad, and that made me feel even more cross with Mum.

'I think Olivia has a right to know, as it affects her,' said Grandad. 'Olivia, your mother has written a letter to the paper, supporting the petition against cadets being set up in the school and complaining about the "creeping militarization" of society.'

'Oh no,' I said. I felt sick. I could barely believe

this. Or what it meant. Everyone at school would know my mum was a peace activist. And the only way I could make sure people didn't take it out on me was to say how much I disagreed with Mum. But for some reason, I just didn't want to do that. I could disagree with her in my head. I could be angry and cross with her − but it wasn't any else's business. I didn't want to have to disagree with her in public, to make people accept me. I wanted my feelings about pacifism − and about Mum − to be private. And, to be honest, I was still working them out. Riya was right − I might want to join the cadets, but it definitely wasn't simple.

'It's ridiculous,' said Grandad. 'Most people who are in the cadets don't go on to join the army − ask anyone. This is scaremongering, and distorting things. I've a good mind to write in myself.'

'Andrew, please don't. That won't help,' said Gran.

'We should have healthy debate, Ruth.'

'I'm not sure all this *is* healthy,' said Gran. 'Not for our family, at any rate. Not for Olivia. Look what has happened so far. Thank you, Olivia dear,' she added, taking the potatoes and putting them in the saucepan.

The only good thing about the situation was

that Gran seemed to want to make a fuss of me and we had a more normal evening. Grandad went out for a meeting, but Gran stayed in and we watched a comedy together and ate popcorn, and then I went up to do some art homework.

That was the night when Gran came up and sat on my bed, and said all the stuff about Dad and how he was so young when I was born, and how much he loved me. And how I should try to talk to him more.

Which – now I have got to know Dad better, and can appreciate the fact he is outside all this fuss – I can see was good advice.

Chapter Twenty-four

I got dressed and went downstairs to find Dad sorting through more of the books from the box. There were magazines and a yellowing page from a newspaper, with an article about cricket and a picture of a man. He looked so familiar that all my other thoughts faded away.

'Who is that man?' I said

'Sir Oliver Lodge,' said Dad. 'There are some books by him in the box too.'

'But . . .' I felt a bit sick suddenly. The picture of him was really old. 'So, he wrote books . . .'

'Yes. He was a professor of physics at Birmingham University, but I'm interested in him because he may well have visited here. He was a friend of Mrs Lutyens, who was the wife of the architect who restored Lindisfarne Castle and who spent a lot of time here.'

'Mrs Lutyens, who was here in Edwardian times?' I said, my heart beating faster.

'Yes,' Dad replied. 'She was a very keen spiritualist – someone who believed you could make contact with the dead. Spiritualism was very popular around the time of the First World War, as so many young men had been killed. This Professor Lodge you see here wrote a famous book, *Raymond, or Life and Death*, after his son Raymond was killed in the war. It's all about how the dead lived in a world just like ours, and how they could eat and drink and smoke, and drink beer, just like they did when they were alive. People were shocked he said people drank beer in heaven. I always thought it was rather touching, myself. He just wanted his boy to still be able to do his favourite things.'

It was true, then. I had met Mrs Lutyens and Professor Lodge in 1916. I had been in 1916, with William! I had no idea how, but it hadn't been a dream.

I knew what I had to ask next.

'Would there have been someone called William at the castle in 1916?' I said.

'William? Well, there was a Billy – short for William – Congreve. He was the boy Edward

236

Hudson wanted to leave Lindisfarne Castle to. But he was killed in 1916.'

'He was killed?'

Dad nodded. 'In the Battle of the Somme in July 1916.'

'In July? He was killed in July?'

'Yes. I actually have his diary, if you would like to look at it. He was an incredibly brave man. He was more and more shocked by the suffering of the soldiers he saw, but he kept fighting and was awarded the Victoria Cross for gallantry. Before he was killed himself, he often risked his life – going to save the wounded on the battlefield.'

What was happening to me? How could I have gone back in time? How could William be dead?

My heart actually hurt. It felt like it was breaking, the way I had only read about in books before. I couldn't bear it. I felt tears rolling down my cheeks and started to sob.

'Olivia!' said Dad. He came over and gave me a big hug. 'Why are you so upset?'

'He was so young. He was so young to die.' My voice wobbled.

'Well, sadly, Olivia, not really,' said Dad. 'Thousands and thousands died, who were younger.

The vast majority of the country believed in the war. Even boys as young as twelve wanted to join the army, and lied about their age in order to fight for their country.'

'Yes, but William was only eighteen,' I cried.

'No, Olivia. Billy Congreve was twenty-five when he died – though I still think that is too young. He left behind a wife, who gave birth to their daughter after he died.'

I wiped my eyes and looked at him.

'So Billy Congreve wasn't eighteen in 1916?'

'No, what gave you that idea?'

'I don't know,' I said. I wasn't sure what to think now. What to do. What had happened to my William, then, in the end?

'You look terrible, Olivia,' said Dad. 'You're as white as a sheet. Are you sure you don't want to go back to bed? You've had such a lot happen these last days. I'm sorry, I'm so used to the history of the place I've forgotten how distressing the details are. You're right to remind me. It *was* terribly sad, and just because it happened so long ago doesn't make it less so.'

For a moment, I considered telling Dad what had happened the night before with William at the castle . . . But there was no way I could see to explain it. I could hardly say, 'By the way, Dad, that William I keep meeting? You don't have to worry about him being older than me. He's a ghost. And if you want to know anything about Lindisfarne Castle in 1916, just ask me. I've been there.'

'No,' I said, 'I think I just need some fresh air. I'll go for a walk, Dad. I'll take Stan.'

'That dog will miss you so much when you go,' laughed Dad. 'He doesn't get as many walks when he is only with me.' He touched me on the arm. 'Are you sure you are OK, Olivia? Take your phone, and ring me if you feel unwell.'

'Thanks, Dad,' I said, and gave him a hug. That was the one good thing about everything that was happening. Things were so much easier with Dad.

But nothing else was.

I had another little weep as soon as I got out of the door. It was probably the shock, more than anything else. Then I looked at Stan.

'I don't know how you do it, Stan, but come on – take me to William,' I said, as we set off down the path. Stan pulled me along, and I looked for signs that things were different. I couldn't see any tourists, but the tide was in now and any daytime visitors would have left the island, so that didn't necessarily mean we had gone back in time. I could see cars in the car park, so that proved we were still in the present. Instead of turning right to the street and then left up to the castle, this time Stan pulled me left, and at the bottom of the road dragged me right, down past a farm. There were hens in the road and sheep in the fields and sparrows in the hedges, but Stan paid no attention. He was on a mission. We powered on up the dunes, and along the shore, practically running round to the cliffs of Cove Haven.

And then, there is William.

'Hello,' I say. It feels really wonderful to see him, now I know the truth. Strange, but wonderful. I should feel overwhelmed, or scared, or even sad, but actually I just feel so glad to see him again. So glad and so, so lucky to be able to see him again at all. Somehow the gap between past and present has melted away, and it is just so good to be with this boy, whatever time we are in.

'Hello,' he says, a little shyly, patting Stan, who rolls over on to his back.

We both crouch down and tickle Stan's tum. We seem to tickle him for ages, not being able to think what to say. William breaks the silence.

'So, Professor Lodge was right, then,' says William. 'You're a ghost. I can hardly believe it.'

'Hardly!' I say indignantly. 'I mean, I'm not dead. Just from over a hundred years in your future.'

William shakes his head in amazement, then we look at each other and burst out laughing.

'This is so weird,' I say. 'And yet it feels so normal, being with you.'

Stan turns his head and licks my hand, and then William's hand. We both laugh again.

'This is the strangest thing I have ever experienced,' says William. 'Do you . . . do you have a message for me, Olivia? That's what Professor Lodge said I was to ask you, if I met you again.'

'I don't know,' I say.

There is a pause. We keep stroking Stan.

'I suppose . . . you may be an answer to prayer,' says William at last. He is serious now. 'If you come from the future, then you must know the past. My future . . . Do you know what happens to me? Do you know if I become a soldier, if I will kill anyone? If I will die in war?'

I think how brave that is of him. To not try to avoid the truth. To face things head-on like that.

'I don't, William. I don't know anything about you. I do know that the war ends in 1918 and that many people die, but I don't know if you die in the war or not. I can try to find out if you like,' I say. 'My dad is a history lecturer.'

It seems very odd to be coolly talking about William dying like this, but here, happy in his company, with him beside me in the past/present, I don't feel upset any more at all. Above us the sky is blue, with white clouds. A bird – I think it is a fulmar – flies above us. Down below, the sea sparkles in the sunlight of a century before mine. And the sun is warm, and William seems as alive as I am. He *is* as alive as I am. We have crossed the divide between our times, and it feels right.

'I got this letter today,' says William. He passes me a piece of paper. 'I wrote to my sister about Christian pacifists, about my love of our country and how I wanted to give my life for it, but had my worries about killing people. About it being on my conscience as a Christian, to kill. I even said that perhaps I might offer my services as a war artist rather than take life. Her husband is a priest. I thought they could advise me.'

I open it. It starts with an address – some vicarage in Norfolk – and 'Dear William,' as you would expect, but how it goes on shocks me.

What has happened to you, my dear brother?

Do you want to bring shame on the family? To break our parents' hearts and those of our dear uncle and aunt, who have lost their only son? Is this the way you honour them, and your cousin's memory?

There can be no such thing as a Christian conscience that refuses to follow Christ into battle against Evil, which stands by and sees British values destroyed, and steps back to let our enemies defeat us. Therefore, there can be no such thing as Christian pacifism.

Furthermore, dear William, as Sidney points out, what does an eighteen-year-old know of conscience? You are too young. All you should care about is your duty, and we trust that you will do it. All your conscience should tell you is to obey orders from those whom God has placed above you.

And finally, dear brother, Sidney says to put out of your head any ridiculous thoughts that

your art can contribute. You are no Muirhead Bone. It is by the gun, not the paintbrush, that we will win the war.
    Your loving sister,
    Elizabeth

'That's a horrible letter, William,' I say. 'And that's rubbish. Pacifism isn't cowardly and there *is* such a thing as Christian pacifism. Your sister and brother-in-law don't know what they are talking about. My mum isn't a Christian, but she is in prison for acting on her beliefs in peace, and refusing to say she was wrong to do so. She's with a nun and a Quaker. So all that about Christian pacifism isn't true.'

I am surprised at how cross I feel. How defensive I feel of Mum and the others.

'So if there is pacifism, is there still war in the future, then?' says William sadly.

'Yes. There is still war.'

'And people are still going to prison for refusing to fight?' he says.

'Well, there is no conscription in our country, but I think there are other countries where that happens,' I say. 'And other countries where people can go to prison for speaking out.'

He goes quiet, and I try to think of how I can help. 'Look, tell me your name. All I know is that you are called William. I'll try to find out, and tell you what happens. Maybe that is what I am meant to do.'

'My name is William –' he begins, but then my phone rang and drowned out his words.

Chapter Twenty-five

It was Dad ringing me. 'Are you all right, Olivia?' he said. 'You've been gone quite a long time.'

'I'm fine, Dad. I'm over at the cliffs at Cove Haven,' I said. I turned to look at William but he had vanished. It was just me and Stan again. The sea looked the same, and up in the air a fulmar spread its wings and rode the currents, but I was back in the present.

'Maybe come home now, Olivia? There is something in the newspaper I want to show you,' Dad said. 'Something to do with Mum.'

'Is she OK?' I said. My heart suddenly started beating faster.

'Yes, Mum is fine,' said Dad, but I had a feeling he wasn't telling me everything.

I walked Stan back to the house quickly. There wasn't anything I could do about William, and it was all I could do to try not to worry about what Dad was going to tell me. He sounded strange, tense on the phone.

Stan and I walked in and Dad was there in the kitchen, a newspaper spread out on the table for me to see.

Links to Pakistan for Foiled London Bomb Plot, said the main headline. The article was about how terrorists in Pakistan had been working with people in London to plan to detonate a bomb at rush hour. Luckily, the intelligence services had been given a tip-off and the men involved had been arrested.

'What has that got to do with Mum?' I said.

Dad pointed further down the page, to where there was a picture of Mum and Johnny, and a smaller paragraph.

Peace activist's Pakistan links. School torn apart as children targeted by pacifist campaign. Time to come down hard, says local MP.

I sat down and read on.

Caz Wilding, the activist recently arrested for inflicting criminal damage at her local army base, has been revealed to be involved in a campaign that is tearing her daughter's school apart. Ms Wilding is not only behind a petition to stop the school having an army cadet group, but has been revealed to have links to Pakistan extremists. A parent at the school has told this paper that Johnny Fitzherbert, Ms Wilding's boyfriend, has hidden links with Pakistan. This paper has further uncovered that Mr Fitzherbert's mother, Dr Akira Fitzherbert, has family ties to a recently arrested hardline fundamentalist preacher in Lahore, Pakistan, and that these cousins have recently been over in Britain.

'This would not surprise me at all,' says local MP, Peter Talbot. 'I believe terrorist sympathizers are infiltrating our so-called peace movements and trying to influence our children against the army, and quite frankly, our brave soldiers have had enough. It's time to show that we will have no tolerance for those who are undermining our military.'

In a further twist to the story, Caz Wilding's father-in-law – Major Andrew Harvey, decorated veteran of Afghanistan – has been involved in setting up the very detachment Ms Wilding is petitioning against and her daughter is known to have applied to join.

'I don't understand,' I said. 'Johnny and his mum

aren't terrorists. How could anyone think that?'

'Johnny has been on the phone to me,' said Dad. 'The police have reassured him that neither he nor his mother are in any trouble or considered to be linked with terrorism. Apparently the connection with the hate preacher is a very remote one, by some distant cousin who married the hate preacher's cousin. It has nothing to with the cousins who were visiting from Pakistan, and Johnny's mother is well known and well regarded in the community. But, the trouble is, the press are out for blood, and are printing details they know will rile their readers and mislead them. People say there is no smoke without fire – even when the fire is based on lies.'

I felt sick.

'Your local MP is trying to stir things up. He is calling for your mum and the other protestors to be seen as terrorist sympathizers. He's suggesting they are in a conspiracy to damage our country's security, and they should be given long prison sentences as a result. It's nonsense, of course. It won't happen, Olivia – but it is frightening how much hate is being stirred up. It's a good job Johnny's father is rich and well connected – his lawyers have written to the newspaper to say that they must retract the lies they are spreading – but, as the saying goes, mud sticks.' Dad must see my worried face, because he adds quickly, 'There's absolutely no proof to these wild claims, Olivia, so your mum can't possibly be imprisoned for them. The rumours are all unfounded, of course, but the MP seems keen to connect it all with having a cadet group in your school.'

Dad looked thoughtful.

'Do you know which parent might have told the newspaper about Johnny's links to Pakistan?'

My heart thundered. 'I think it's Chloe and her family.'

Dad frowned. 'How does she know Johnny?'

'I think I told her that his family come from Pakistan,' I said. Actually I didn't *think* I had, I knew I had told her

'Why?' said Dad.

'I don't know,' I said. 'It all seems so stupid now. I was just cross about everything. I'd had a row at school, and then I went to a barbecue with Chloe and when I came home I had a row with Johnny and Mum. I rang Chloe and told her all about it; all about them and how fed up I was. I didn't mean anything by it. I just knew Chloe would be sympathetic, because her family are really cross about the petition, and . . .'

I stopped. There was no going back, if I told Dad any more. He'd hear all about the whole mess. How bad it was with Mum. How rubbish I'd been. I looked at him, through my tears. He just opened his arms for a hug. I leant against him, and let his warmth steady me.

I couldn't stand being alone with it all any more. I kept rerunning the conversations in my head, and my thoughts only ever went round and round. Dad had been really listening to me these last days, and he was clearly brilliant at sifting through things and looking at both sides, to get to the heart of the matter. I needed Dad to help me sort things out. I could see everyone's point of view, but I couldn't see my own any more.

'I get the feeling there's a lot going on here,' Dad said. 'You can tell me anything, Olivia.'

So I did. Everything that had happened at school, right up to Mum's letter in the *Gazette*. And what happened next.

Chapter Twenty-six

It was the Friday of summer half-term. The night before Mum went and cut a hole in the fence at the military base and put flowers in it. It was Chloe's birthday. She was planning a family barbecue that evening, and she'd invited me and Nola and Riya.

I was hopeful. Chloe inviting Riya was a big step towards them patching things up. But at lunchtime, worry was chewing away at me again. I walked into our form room to see Nola talking with Riya. My heart sank when I heard what they were talking about.

'Of course the petition is to do with Eddie,' said Nola, who was crying. 'Eddie was in the army and Chloe says the people behind the petition want to stop people being in the army.'

'No, they don't, Nola,' said Riya patiently. 'They just don't want schools to have army cadet groups.'

'But I still don't understand why,' said Nola.

'Because they think it isn't a suitable thing to happen in a school,' said Riya.

'But why not?' said Nola.

'For one thing, as we are finding out, it makes normal school life difficult for students who, for any number of reasons, don't agree with the idea of the army. It excludes people.'

'Rubbish,' said Chloe, going over to them. 'I'm not in the cricket team. I don't feel like that has made things difficult for me, like I'm being excluded in any way by the school.'

'But it isn't about something as simple as cricket,' said Riya. 'People don't mind if you don't like cricket. But some people will see someone not wanting to join the cadets as being about more than just cadets – that the person is saying they don't want to fight for their country, that they don't want to join the army.'

'Well, that's right. You *should* want to join the army,' said Tyler, butting in.

I couldn't stand it any more. People were being so dense, and Tyler was so irritating. I just had to say something. 'I don't think everyone should have to join the army,' I said. 'Just that it is fine if you do.'

'Exactly!' said Chloe, but I didn't see how I was agreeing with her. I was just disagreeing with Tyler.

'We shouldn't have to make that important decision in front of people at school though,' said Riya. 'It's too much pressure. Look at how people, like Seb, are making others feel like cowards if they say they don't want to join the cadets. And another thing – soldiers aren't meant to question orders, right? Part of the objection to all this is the idea that if children join the cadets, they will get used to obeying orders and forget that it is OK to ask questions – including about whether wars are right or wrong.'

'That's ridiculous. Learning to be disciplined won't turn us into zombies, Riya,' I say. 'I'm just as capable of deciding whether things are right or wrong, whether I am in cadets or not.'

'But cadets is part of the army, and about what the army stands for,' said Riya. 'You have to basically agree with fighting, if you are in cadets.'

'But why wouldn't someone agree with fighting for our country?' said Nola.

'If you don't agree with killing people,' said Riya. 'Like pacifists don't.'

'Nobody is teaching anyone to kill people in cadets, Riya,' I said. 'Don't be silly. You don't even have to join the army afterwards.'

'No, but you are being shown in school, by people

in army uniform, how to do things you do in the army, and yet it won't be emphasized that in the real army, the difference is that you have to be prepared to kill people,' said Riya. 'That's not silly — that's a fact. Maybe it is right to kill to defend your country, but all the objectors are saying is that you have to accept that joining the army isn't like any other school club or job — it is going to be a very serious decision you should get to make on your own, without any sort of pressure — and you shouldn't just drift into it or be sort of brainwashed because you enjoyed cadets at school and everyone else is doing it.'

'I don't think people like my grandad would ever brainwash people,' I said, feeling cross.

'And Eddie didn't join the army just to kill people,' said Nola. 'But people still killed him.' Chloe put her arm around her.

'Don't make it personal, guys,' pleaded Riya. 'This isn't about Eddie, or your grandad, Olivia.'

'Why are you arguing with us, then?' said Chloe. 'Are you becoming a Quaker too?'

'No, but I agree with the petition,' said Riya. 'I think it is fine if people want to join the cadets *after* school, but cadets shouldn't be run in school time, so that it feels like any other thing we learn here. And in an army town like this, with all the people who are likely to want to join the cadets, it will make it feel more normal to join in and make it more likely there will be a big fuss if you don't want to. It messes up the school community. Look at how horrible people are being to Aidan and his parents – people aren't respecting each other any more.'

'That's not our fault,' I say. Although I felt a twinge. It wasn't my fault he was getting picked on, but it didn't feel right that I wasn't helping him against being bullied.

'Nobody is making him join,' said Seb, getting involved as usual. 'So why does he need to object?' Seb clearly hadn't taken in what Riya had been saying, but turned on her anyway. 'And why are you fighting his battles for him anyway? Do you fancy him?'

'You're pathetic. She isn't fighting any battles for me,' said Aidan, coming into the room. 'Just change the subject.'

'I'll change the subject when your parents stop that stupid petition,' said Seb. 'If people are being nasty to them, they deserve it. We're not all cowards.'

'Your family is ruining everything,' said Chloe to Aidan.

Aidan shrugged. He was looking really tired. I felt really bad. He'd only just come back to school, and already the atmosphere was clearly wearing him down. He wasn't someone who liked being the centre of attention and, thanks to Seb, people who really wanted to join the cadets were getting cross with him everywhere, on and offline – there was nowhere he could get away from it. I bit my lip. I could understand how he felt. But at least I could choose to keep out of it, keep under the radar. I was – and everyone at school took it for granted I was – still pro-cadets, so nobody was going to be angry with me for my position, and I hadn't said anything about understanding the other side. He had made his position against cadets clear, and now there was nowhere to hide, even if he wanted to. That was hard. Once you started taking a stand, then you couldn't go back. And what stand could I take, when I could see both sides?

'That's so unfair,' said Riya. She was being really strong. 'Aidan and his family haven't ruined anything. Anyway, it isn't just Aidan's family who have signed. My parents have too. They think army cadets in itself is fine, but it should be done outside school time.'

'Well, your parents aren't British, are they?' said Tyler.

I gasped. This was horrible.

'I beg your pardon?' said Riya. She looked really shocked and angry.

'Aren't you Muslims or something?'

'No, we're Hindus. But what's that got to do with anything? They are British citizens and I was born here.'

'Yes, Tyler,' I said. 'Riya's parents have a right to sign the petition, even if we don't agree with it.'

I was glad I said that, anyway. I didn't know what to say about Aidan, but I couldn't just stand by and let Tyler say that to my best friend, and I knew he didn't want to row with me, because of Grandad.

Instead he shrugged and went off.

'Thanks, Olivia,' Riya said. She looked at me kind of intensely, and I guessed she was waiting for me to say more about how my mum had signed too, but I didn't say anything else. I didn't agree with Mum, so why should I have to get into rows because of her opinions?

We had registration and I tried to focus on double chemistry. Before I knew it, it was time to go home. Riya waited for me in the corridor.

'Olivia, thanks for sticking up for me against Tyler, but why aren't you admitting your mum is involved with the petition too?' said Riya. 'She's even more involved than Aidan's parents now. She's got loads of people to sign – she even rang my parents. It isn't fair that you are letting Aidan's family take all the blame. Seb is using it to get everyone worked up against Aidan.'

'It isn't fair if the blame comes to me when I don't agree with Mum,' I said. 'I think it is fine to have army cadets here.'

'It's not just about that any more,' said Riya. 'Aidan needs people to stick up for him, to say that he has a right to his opinion, and people will listen to you, Olivia. Everyone loves your grandad and knows you want to do cadets. You know, more than anyone, that there are two sides to this problem. If you don't stand up and help stop this hate, then you are the coward.'

Then she walked off. I let her go.

Chapter Twenty-seven

Riya had made me really angry. I was already feeling bad about things. She hadn't helped. It wasn't anything to do with me if Aidan's family were getting targeted. How would telling everyone about Mum change how people felt about Aidan's family?

We were all supposed to go together to Chloe's after school, but Riya walking off had changed things. She had left a birthday card and a present by Chloe's locker and a note.

Hope you have a good party.
    Probably better if I don't come tonight, as we might just argue.
    Riya

'I don't care,' said Chloe, when she came to her locker. But you could tell she did.

I was glad Riya wasn't coming. What did she want me to do? I wasn't the one bullying Aidan. I hated that this cadets thing was such a big issue for everyone, anyway. I was sorry Aidan was looking so tired, and about the nasty letters and the graffiti, but it wasn't my fault if his parents were against the school having cadets. And it was nothing to do with me if my mum was supporting the petition or, knowing Mum, leading the campaign. So it wasn't fair to mix me up in it. I was fed up of Riya looking disappointed with me. Of Gran looking worried. Of not hearing from Mum. It made me feel I was doing something wrong, and I wasn't. Why did I have to take sides?

So when I got to the barbecue and Chloe's parents were so pleased to see me, it was really nice. People were laughing. Chloe's mum and dad had their arms around each other and were dancing to music. There was a smell of burgers, and bright salads were in bowls on tables, and people were smiling and just being normal.

'Sorry to hear about all the trouble you are having with those people's petition, love,' said Chloe's mum, swishing away from the dancing and giving me a big hug. She was so soft and warm and cuddly, I could almost forgive her for bringing it up.

'I'm on your grandad's side. Chloe's been telling us all about it.'

The trouble was, I wasn't sure if Chloe was getting it right. The petition wasn't about Grandad. Or me. But I didn't try to explain. It just seemed like too much work. I wanted to have fun. And I liked being liked. I liked Chloe and I liked being liked by her and her family. What was wrong with that?

And then Seb's family came over, with this friend of theirs they had brought along. A woman I didn't know. She was really pretty and very friendly – easy to talk to.

'So what do you think about this petition then, girls?' she said, bringing her plate over and sitting next to me and Chloe. I tried not to show on my face how fed up I was that we were talking about it again. 'Bit of a fuss about nothing, or something more important?' She asked us as if she really cared about what we thought, as if our opinions counted. I found myself wishing that Mum had asked me what I really thought more, instead of telling me, or taking it for granted. Maybe if she had done that, I'd know my own mind a bit more. This woman was really interested. It felt good having an adult really listen. 'Maybe it's nothing to do with you, though. I bet you aren't really involved.'

'Oh, we are!' I remember Chloe saying. 'At least, Olivia is. Her grandad is an army major and he wants to help set up cadets at school. But Olivia even had to move out of home because her mum and her boyfriend are against it.'

That made me feel squirmy inside. This was me and my mum she was talking about. To a stranger, however nice.

'It's awful for her,' Chloe continued. 'Olivia wants to be a cadet and her mum won't let her. Her mum has even started a petition against cadets. Olivia's had to be really brave and take a stand against her family. Not her grandad, of course – he's a war hero. But she has to stand against her mum. I'm so proud of her. My whole family is. It must be really hard having a mum who's a peace activist.'

Chloe said 'peace activist' as if it was something awful, something to be ashamed of. However sympathetic Chloe was to me, it didn't feel right someone else pitying me for having Mum as my mum. I could feel sorry for myself, but no one else should.

It was all a bit of a shock, really. Of course, Nola and Riya knew Mum. Anyone who had been at primary school with me knew Mum. But I'd deliberately never talked to Chloe about her, so I somehow, stupidly I suppose, had thought she didn't know. I had thought if we didn't talk about it, it wouldn't be an issue. I didn't realize she'd known and been feeling sorry for me all this time. Maybe someone had told Chloe about Mum and the white poppies at school. I suppose I should never have expected that it would have stayed a secret.

So did everyone know, then? Did everyone already know about Mum's involvement? I'd been so worried about saying what I thought about it, and how people would react. I needn't have. I'd kept my head down and let Aidan take all the insults. Was that why nobody had got cross with me? Because they thought I was a brave heroine? It should be a relief, but I didn't like that they all seemed to think they knew what I thought already. How could they know what I thought, when I wasn't sure myself? Did me keeping silent about everything just make it look as if I totally disagreed with Mum and Aidan, that I couldn't see any point at all in what they were saying, in what they were doing? That I was taking a stand against Mum? I was beginning to see how by not saying something, I was still, in effect, saying something – and when I wasn't saying anything, I didn't have control over what people thought my opinion was. That made me feel so fed up. Why did things have to be so complicated? It was all such a mess.

'Really!' said the friendly woman, her eyes opening wide. 'That sounds tough.' She was so smiley and sympathetic. 'Tell me about them . . .'

I told Dad all of it.

'I think that woman must have been a journalist,' I said. 'I wish I hadn't talked to her. But I didn't say anything to her about Johnny's mum being from Pakistan and having cousins visiting, Dad. I didn't even know about that until I went back to Mum's flat after the barbecue, and Mum told me she was going to support the demonstration the next morning. I asked her not to go, but Johnny said it was important – that he would have gone if he wasn't going to meet up with his cousins, who had come over from Pakistan. I thought he was really unhelpful and unfair. I remember telling that to Chloe later on the phone and her being surprised Johnny had cousins from Pakistan when he had such an English name, and that's when I told her that Johnny's mum was from Pakistan.

I don't understand why it has got into such a horrible mess and why it is in the papers. Why are they even reporting about the petition?' I asked. 'It's just about our school having cadets.'

'I think your mum and the others have really rattled some powerful people,' said Dad. 'And this is a way of discrediting them and making their lives harder. There's a lot of money to be made from war and selling arms. And powerful people don't like to lose money.'

'How would people lose money because of Mum?'

'Your mum and the others are making some very good points about modern warfare. People are starting to listen to them. If the government listens, and stops making and selling so many weapons to other countries, then people who own shares in the companies who make the weapons will lose money, and the people employed in the factories making the weapons will lose their jobs.'

'Maybe it would be better to have a job making things other than weapons,' I said.

Dad raised his eyebrow. 'That's a valid point, Olivia, but it doesn't work if you are not a pacifist, like your mum. If you are not a pacifist and you think that there should be an army, then soldiers need weapons, and someone has to make them.'

I nodded. I couldn't help thinking of the posters on Mum's wall about war hurting children. Soldiers needed weapons, but wars still weren't good.

'I suppose you have to be careful about the weapons that are made. Like not making mines and cluster bombs,' I said, remembering the sort of things Mum and her friends talked about at home.

'Yes,' said Dad. 'The worldwide weapons trade could definitely be more ethical about the type of weapons it makes. Anyway,' he continued, 'your mum and the others are saying the most important thing is to stop awful weapons being made and used, but the people who sell weapons, or have shares in the companies who sell them, and the people who worry about their jobs, say it isn't. The government has to decide what to do, but either way somebody is going to be angry with them. They'd rather the whole argument went away, but they can't ignore this.'

I felt a bit ashamed that I understood about wanting the whole argument to go away. But I knew it hadn't worked for me, and it wouldn't work for the government.

'I still don't understand what this has got to do

with Johnny's cousins and the petition against having cadets in school,' I said.

'Olivia, more and more people are listening to your mum and the others – you can tell by the number of people who have signed the petition, who are talking about this issue. So the people who don't want them to be listened to have started smearing them – spreading lies and half-truths about them, so that others won't like or trust them. It's always been like that. History is full of things like this. You should have seen the propaganda in the First World War – newspapers made people believe that enemy soldiers were monsters with no morals or decency, instead of sons and brothers and husbands, like their own. It made it easier to kill the enemy if you didn't remember they were human, that they were people just like you. These people aren't killing your mum and the others, of course, but they are killing their reputations.'

'So why are they going on about Mum? She is only a gardener.'

'It's not just your mum. Johnny told me the newspaper also ran an untrue story, before, about Sister Mary being cruel when she was a teacher – but so many of her ex-students stuck up for her, they had to issue an apology. So then they moved on to your mum, and now they have their story – a woman with a boyfriend with links to Pakistan, related to a war hero, who is preventing her own daughter from joining the cadets. Even though it is ridiculous, it all creates the impression that what your mum and the others are doing is somehow not patriotic, not British, and stops people listening to her or feeling sympathy for her. And this particular newspaper is only too glad to run this angle on the story, to encourage that to happen.'

I felt sick. It was the thought of so many people lying and twisting things – and telling thousands of people who didn't know her that my lovely mum was someone she wasn't. And there was no way to tell each one of them the truth, or be sure they would listen.

'I'm so sorry, Dad. What can I do? I didn't want to hurt Mum. I love her.'

'I know you do.' Dad gave me a hug.

There was a sound of something dropping through the letterbox, and Dad went to get it.

'Olivia, a letter from your mum,' he said.

I didn't want to open it.

'It won't be about the article,' Dad said quietly. 'She will have written this before that.'

It was still horrible seeing the envelope with her writing on it, and thinking of her being locked away in a prison. And it was horrible knowing that some people wanted her to stay there for a long, long time. And most of all, I felt awful that I had helped them think that.

I opened it.

Dear Olivia,

I never want to hurt you and I am so sorry I went ahead and cut that fence and risked prison. It just felt like the right thing to do, but I was really looking forward to being with you this holiday and perhaps I should have let someone else do it. It's just that this world is so beautiful and fragile, and I want to keep it safe for you. I love you so much. Please forgive me for messing up our time together. I miss you very much and I hope that this Monday we will have good news.

Lots of love,

Mum xx

I found there were tears running down my cheeks. My mum was so brave and so beautiful. And I wanted to hug her so badly. I wanted to see her so much. I loved her more than ever. How could anyone think she was a bad person?

'Dad, why did the MP say that stuff about sympathizing with terrorists? Isn't it clear Mum is against all violence?' I said.

'Well,' Dad replied, 'I've looked him up, and this particular MP makes money from investing in firms that sell weapons, so a politician like that will particularly not like pacifists. He is linking army cadets in school with patriotism, not because he is like your grandad, but so that he can say your mum is unpatriotic for not wanting them in schools, for being against the army. That's a powerful thing to say about a person, when the country is in fear of terrorist attack, because a lot of people will believe that not supporting the army means you are siding with our enemies. And he is deliberately using the word "conspiracy" to suggest that as well as being charged with damaging military property, she should be charged with conspiracy against the government – and that carries a sentence of years in prison.'

'Dad!' I burst into tears. I think it was the worst moment of my life.

Chapter Twenty-eight

'What can I do, Dad?' I said. 'I don't want them to lock Mum away! I don't want them to get away with these horrible lies. I want people to see that Mum is lovely and she loves our country as much as anyone.'

'Oh, Olivia,' said Dad, coming over and putting his arms around me. 'I'm sorry. I didn't mean to get you worried. Nobody will lock Mum away. It is obvious she hasn't done anything remotely to do with terrorism. One crooked politician and one journalist can't put your mum away for years, no matter how much they might want to. They'd need proof of what they are suggesting, and they won't find anything because your mum hasn't done anything – and would never do anything – like that. I'm more worried and angry about how they are destroying her reputation, but you mustn't worry about that either. I got a text from Grandad and Gran when you were out – they are coming back to help clear your mum's name. There are many good, ethical MPs who will help put the record straight too, I am sure. And many more journalists, who care passionately about the truth. We'll think of something. Don't despair, Olivia.'

Stan came over, pushing his cold nose against my hands, putting his front paws on my knees and trying to lick my face. I flung my arms around him and sobbed into his fur.

'It's going to be OK. Really,' Dad said. 'Look, we can't leave the island right now because of the tides, but we can leave early tomorrow and be back at the vicarage to meet up with your gran and grandad and plan what to do next. How about we go to the pub later for some fish and chips?'

Stan gave a woof, and I nodded. I was amazed Dad has remembered that's my favourite meal.

'I'll take Stan out now before we go, then,' I said.

'You sure?' said Dad. 'Don't get too tired.'

Stan scraped at the door to get out, and dragged me along the path. I let him, as I didn't have the energy to pull him back. I felt so tired and depressed. And ashamed. Dad seemed to think we could still help put the record straight about Mum, but it scared me how my words had got twisted, and how people had got so angry and wanted to hurt people who didn't agree with them.

It felt too similar to school. How had something which seemed so simple – having cadets in a school – get so twisted, and used as some weird cause for bullying? That wasn't my idea of what cadets was about at all. And there was Aidan. It was horrible what had happened to his family, how people had turned on them. And I could see, now, it was a lot like what was happening to Mum. Smearing. Riya was right. You couldn't just stand by and let people tell lies about things you love, about people you love. Even if the truth was complicated, even if there was more than one side to every question and you'd rather there weren't, you had to live with that. You had to keep listening to each other, keep being kind, even if you didn't agree, and speak out, even if you didn't like doing that. Otherwise, you ended up living with lies and hate, and they spoil everything. I should have said something to stick up for Aidan, even if I didn't agree with him. I should have done something, not left it to the liars. But what exactly should I have done, and more importantly, what could I do now?

I looked up to see that the tide was in, and people

had left the island for the day. Instead of turning up to the castle, this time Stan pulled me a way we don't normally walk, so that we headed down the road that would take us off the island.

'Where are you going, Stan?' I said, but he kept walking, past the empty car park, and down to the shore, to the place where the Pilgrim's Way walking route ends. A sign explained this was the way people used to come to Lindisfarne before the road was built – a path across the wet sand, marked by wooden poles, that only appears when the tide is out. It was hidden again now by water, and we stood for a moment, looking at the sea, and the tops of the row of posts stretching out of the water, going right back to the mainland. We watched a gull swoop in low, above the white-flecked waves curling in and breaking at our feet. And the sounds of the sea and the wind, and the cries of seabirds, mingled.

And then Stan barks, once, and the bit of the sea we are looking at disappears. The tide is out, the Pilgrim's Way is visible, the footpath clear; the island is no longer divided from the mainland. The posts are stood in the wet sand, fully revealed – the ancient route is uncovered again. And Stan pulls me on to it.

A figure on its own is walking towards us.

'Is it William?' I say, and Stan's plumed tail waves enthusiastically as he rushes forward. Edwardian oystercatchers take flight as we pass, and my feet squelch on the watery surface of the sand.

William's head is down as he strides along towards us, his satchel across his shoulder as usual. Even at a distance I can tell something is wrong, that he is unhappy.

'William!' I call, and his head comes up.

I find myself running, trying not to slip, and I reach him, breathless, Stan excited by our speed.

'William, what's the matter?' I say, as Stan jumps up at him.

William bends down and Stan licks his face. He lifts it and I see he has been crying.

'What's happened?' I say.

He shrugs miserably and, crouching, puts his head down so I can't see his face any more. Stan wriggles low on the sand and keeps licking. William puts his arms around him and kneels fully on the wet sand, burying his face in Stan's fur for a moment, then he rubs his sleeve angrily against his face and stands up.

He still won't look at me, but he puts his hand in his satchel and thrusts three white feathers at me.

'What does this mean?' I say.

'Three girls came up to me in the street in Berwick. They were about your age, Olivia, maybe a little older. They asked me why I wasn't fighting. I told them that I was only seventeen, and they laughed at me. They laughed at me, Olivia. They said I was lying and that I was a coward, and they gave me these feathers in front of everyone. And everybody just stopped and stared.'

He looks so humiliated, so hurt. It makes my heart hurt too. I feel furious at those horrible girls. How dare they bully William?

'That's awful, William,' I say.

'Nobody has ever looked at me with such contempt,' he says. 'I was so angry, so ashamed. It was just as my sister had said in her letter. I thought about my mother and father being sent feathers in the post, should I not fight once I am eighteen. Their shame. The unhappiness I would cause them.

'Then a recruiting officer came round the corner and asked me if I liked being called a coward, and I said I didn't. He told me to go along with him and he would make me feel better, and it was only Professor

Lodge and Mr Hudson coming out of the bank at that moment that stopped me marching to the recruiting office right away. Mr Hudson explained to the sergeant that I would be given a commission after my birthday next week, and that my parents were coming to Lindisfarne this weekend to say goodbye. The recruiting officer saluted and left us. But I swear to you, Olivia, if Mr Hudson and the professor had not come upon us I would have enlisted there and then. And this is what scares me: I would have made the most important decision of my life not because I believed it to be right, but because of three white feathers.'

He strokes Stan and I see his fingers are trembling.

'Where are Professor Lodge and Mr Hudson now?' I say.

'I asked that I could walk on my own, this last part, and so they went on ahead. Did you not see them on your way?'

'No, in my time this is sea. The tide is in. I think it changed so that I could meet you,' I say.

'Look at this, Olivia.' He takes a newspaper out of his bag and gives it to me. The headline reads: *Conscientious Objector Says He Would Rather Be Killed than to Kill.*

'The editor says this is the limit of absurdity, as well as the limit of shirking one's duties,' William says. 'But Olivia, I realize now that this headline is what I believe too. I cannot help it. This is what I understand by obeying the Ten Commandments. I cannot disobey my conscience. Yet three white feathers would have undone me. I would have taken up arms, just to avoid those looks. And if I decide not to go next week, I am scared of standing up and declaring it before people who will look at me in that way, people like my brother-in-law. I am a coward.'

William wasn't a coward. He knew how horrible the papers would be – like the papers who were being so mean about Mum – but he still wanted to do the right thing. He was just scared. And he admitted it. To me that made him braver – for wanting to do the right thing for the right reasons.

'You're not a coward at all, William. I've never met a braver, gentler boy,' I say. 'I don't know anyone who tries to do the right thing as much as you.'

William laughs a little sadly. 'I'm sure you can't say that, Olivia. As you say, I am sure there are people in your time who try to do the right thing.'

He is right. I think of Mum in prison, and her beautiful letter. I think of Sister Mary and all the other peace activists. I think of Gran, and Grandad; so brave when he went to Afghanistan, and of Nola's Eddie and her uncle too. And I think of Dad and Johnny. All of them, trying to do the right thing. And then I think of that journalist, and that MP, and the girls with the white feathers, and the people making money from weapons, and the people who own the newspapers that tell lies and smear people and stir up hate and confusion – all at different times in history, but always with the same horrible result. I think of cowards like that turning kind people like Chloe and Nola against other kind people, like Riya and Aidan. And I think of Aidan especially, who is as brave as William, in his own way. Aidan, my friend, who I have let down. And I feel ashamed.

'You're right. It looks like there are good and bad people in both times,' I say.

'I still do not know what to do, Olivia. I still don't know if the right thing is to enlist. I love my country. I could say I will not kill, but I will serve as an ambulance driver, but then I am patching people up just so we can send them back into war again.'

'It is still dangerous for you,' I say.

'It's not as dangerous as losing my soul by breaking God's holy commandment, is it?' he says.

'I'm not scared of danger, Olivia. Well, maybe I am, but I would rather face danger than never see God because I have killed another man.'

I know William is telling the truth. He really believes what he says. Grandad would love this boy so much.

We walk along in silence for a while.

'I've been finding out things. There are conscientious objectors called absolutists,' William says. 'They oppose war totally – absolutely, for religious or political reasons. They say that only everybody refusing to take part in wars will stop it. They even refuse to put on a uniform and work in the army, in any way, as it would still help soldiers kill and be killed.'

'I think my mum would be one of those,' I say.

'They say that the prisons the absolutists are sent to are dark and damp, that the absolutists are beaten, and some, since they refuse to put on uniform, are left naked,' William says. 'But even more than this, Olivia, they say they are going to be shot.'

'That's terrible,' I say. I've never heard of this. Nobody mentioned this when we went on our First World War school trip to Ypres.

'Whatever I choose to do, Olivia,' William says,

'I may die in this war. I may die as a soldier, I may die as an ambulance driver, I may be shot as an absolutist. I just want to die well.'

I feel like a cloud of sadness and tiredness has settled over me. I know I am walking along with a boy who died before I was born, but I can't bear the idea that he will die so young, in confusion, or in pain, or in shame, not knowing if he has done the right thing.

'Would you like me to find out what happens to you?' I say. 'I can do some research, I can look you up. I can come back and tell you what happens. Help you decide.'

William doesn't reply for a while. We keep walking. I look up at the sky. The clouds make beautiful, strange patterns in every century.

'I don't think you can tell me what happens in the future, Olivia,' says William slowly, turning to me, his eyes serious and kind. 'I don't think I'd want to know, even if you could. I think I have to make this decision now, in my present. That's the time I live in, I pray in. My life on this earth will have ended before yours begins. Nothing you find out will change that. I understand now that it is not about how or when I die – it's about how I choose to live. I must write my own story.'

I look over at him as we walk along. We reach the end of the Pilgrim's Way and come up the shore. He smiles at me. He looks so much better, so at peace.

'Thank you, Olivia,' William says. 'Thank you for listening. You have helped me so much. I know what I shall do now.'

We stop, and he opens his arms, and we hug tight. I feel his warmth, the tweed of his jacket, but inside I feel much more – I feel his goodness, his gentleness, his sensitivity, his fear, but also his courage and his love.

'Goodbye, Olivia,' he whispers, and kisses me on the cheek.

And then he is gone.

I was standing by the sea with Stan. A gull swooped overhead and cried into the air.

Chapter Twenty-nine

Dad drove us back home the next day. As soon as we got back to the vicarage, I knew what I had to do. I hadn't stopped thinking about things since I'd last seen William, and I'd finally come to some decisions. I wasn't looking forward to acting on them, but I had to be brave.

I rang Aidan.

His mum answered the phone. Her voice sounded tired and worried, not as warm as it normally was.

'Hello?' she said suspiciously.

'Hello, it's Olivia,' I said.

'Olivia love!' she said, friendly as usual. I felt really guilty. Aidan obviously hadn't told her how I had let him down, how I had stood by and let him be bullied and had done nothing. I wished I had stuck up for him. I wished I had stuck up for her and Aidan's dad, stood up for the people I always knew were good –

even if I disagreed with them – instead of trying to keep out of trouble. 'You poor love. It's all so nasty. Your poor mum. And these awful journalists . . . I thought you might be one of them ringing again. How are you?'

'I'm OK,' I said. 'Is Aidan there?'

'Of course. I'll get him. I believe we'll be seeing you later, anyway. I can't get a babysitter, so your grandad has suggested we should all meet here for a council of war – maybe not the best of terms for a Quaker, but I get his point! Anyway, I'll get Aidan. He'll be so pleased you rang.'

I doubted it.

'Hello?' said Aidan, cautiously.

'Hello, it's Olivia,' I said unnecessarily, as I'd just heard his mum tell him who was calling.

'I know,' he said. His voice didn't get any friendlier. I took a deep breath. I thought of William. I had to do the right thing. No matter how scary it was.

'Look, Aidan. I just want to say I'm sorry. I'm sorry I didn't stick up for you at school, and I'm sorry about the petition and cadets and everything. I know I was wrong to not get involved, to not fight for you. Riya told me I was being a coward and I should have listened to her. But now Mum is in such trouble, and I have an idea that I think could help everyone, if we all get together. Can I come round to talk to you, when Grandad and Gran and Dad go to your house?'

There was a pause.

'OK,' he says. 'And I am sorry about your mum, Olivia.'

'Thank you. I am too,' I say. 'And . . . thanks for giving me a chance.'

'Hmm,' he says. He doesn't sound too sure about it. This wasn't going to be easy. But maybe I didn't deserve it to be. I remembered William, and how hurt those girls had made him, and how angry I had been when he told me about them. It was easy to feel angry and want to defend William against those girls – those girls I didn't know – but I hadn't exactly rushed in to stick up for Aidan at school, against my own classmates. Not like Riya.

Next I rang Riya. She picked up straight away.

'Riya, it's me, Olivia. I'm so sorry,' I said. 'You were right. I'm sorry I didn't do anything to try to stop all this craziness.'

Silence.

'Say something!'

'That's OK,' she said at last. It was such a relief

to hear her. She didn't sound like her usual friendly self, but at least she was speaking to me. Accepting my apology. This was hard, but I was glad I was doing it. I needed to do it.

'Thanks so much,' I said. I meant it. 'And I really need your help. I've got to stop the awful stories about Mum.'

'I'm sorry about the horrible things the newspapers are saying about your mum, Olivia. Everyone is. Even Chloe,' said Riya. She was much more friendly now, warm even. Riya was such a good person. She really cared about people and about doing the right thing. I wished I could introduce her to William. My heart twisted a bit at the thought of him, but it also gave me strength.

'Chloe and her family caused a lot of the problem,' I said. 'They spoke to the press and made Mum and Johnny and his mum out to be terrorist sympathizers, even though it isn't true. Mum and Johnny hate violence in any form – they are only trying to work for peace. That's all they have ever tried to do.'

Riya sighed. 'To be fair, Olivia, Chloe's family probably didn't know it would all get so out of hand. She told me your gran and grandad went over this morning and talked to them, and her family are really sorry. That journalist friend of Seb's family got them really scared and they ended up thinking they were foiling a terrorist attack by telling her everything they knew about Johnny. They are really angry with Seb's family now. They say they don't want anything more to do with them.'

'Why did they talk about the petition, though? Why did they go on about conspiracy and wanting Mum to be in prison for years?'

'They didn't — that was Seb's dad and the MP and the journalist. Honestly, Olivia, Chloe was crying today. She messaged me and then I rang her and found all this out. You know what she's like. She'd do anything to make it up with you, but she feels really stupid and she's scared. Please forgive her.'

Riya was wonderful. I was so lucky to have such a good friend, to know such a good person.

'Well, you forgave me so I can hardly argue with that,' I said. 'And actually, if Chloe really does want to make a difference, she could be a big help. Do you think she would come over to Aidan's at four o'clock? Gran and Grandad and Dad are meeting the Brocklesbys then . . .'

'I can ask her,' says Riya.

I texted Nola too, telling her about my plan, and

got a message from Riya letting me know she and Chloe would be there.

Aidan's mum was so nice to us when we all arrived. I'd called ahead to check it would be OK if the four of us turned up. Chloe was really nervous and had brought a big bunch of flowers.

'This is from my mum and dad,' she said, her eyes anxious and pleading when she looked nervously up at Aidan's mum. 'We're so sorry and we will do anything to make things better.' I could tell it took real courage.

'It's all right, Chloe. I've had a long talk to Olivia's gran and grandad, who have set the record straight about all this,' said Aidan's mum. 'But thank you so much, these are beautiful.' She gave her a kiss. Chloe looked so relieved. I had forgotten how lovely her smile was.

'I'll bring you up some popcorn or something,' Aidan's mum said. 'At least this has got Aidan to tidy his room.' It seemed funny to hear Aidan's mum talking about normal things like popcorn and untidy rooms, when everything was still so bad.

'We're having a meeting down here and we are

going to sort something out to help your mum,' Aidan's mum said to me. 'Your grandad says he is trying to talk to some sympathetic MPs across the parties, and to people behind the scenes in government, and your dad knows some really good journalists who care about the truth and are very sympathetic to us. We are trying to put together a story the newspapers will be interested in, and get the truth known.'

I was glad, but I had my own ideas too, and I couldn't wait to go upstairs and share them with the others.

It was a bit awkward when we got up to Aidan's room and he opened the door and we came face to face. Chloe was brave again and rushed to speak first.

'I'm sorry, Aidan. My family are really sorry. Please forgive us. We got it all wrong.' Her voice wobbled a bit at the end, and I saw her blink back tears.

Aidan frowned and ran his fingers through his hair.

'I'm sorry too, Aidan,' I said. I couldn't let Chloe do it all. 'I just want to tell you again, to your face. I was a coward, I see that. I should have spoken up more. I understood what you were doing much more than Chloe and her family, but I didn't say anything. I'm worse than Chloe really, because I knew you better. Please say you forgive us both.'

I put my arm around Chloe's shoulders. She was shaking a little, and I admired her even more. She was really sorry. That was obvious. I hoped Aidan could see it as clearly as the rest of us. Nola and Riya had moved closer to Chloe. We were on the landing outside Aidan's room, willing him to let us in.

'I want to help put things right,' I continued.

Aidan had stopped frowning and was looking at me now, a serious expression on his face, as if he was trying to decide whether to believe me. I could see, looking into his eyes – so sincere and kind, like William's – more than ever how much I had hurt him, and I felt truly terrible. We had known each other for years. I had spent holidays with him and his lovely family. I knew he was a good and kind person. Why on earth had I ever thought it was all right to keep out of the school arguments? By not doing anything I had done something – I had said that it was fine for Seb to bully him, for people to spread rumours. I had let the haters win.

'I'm so ashamed. I'm so, so sorry. Please, let us in, Aidan. I've got a plan,' I said.

He bit his lip and looked at me and Chloe. Chloe gave a little sob and a big sniff and then, unexpectedly, a hiccup.

'Sorry!' she said, and we all laughed.

Aidan smiled, and it was such a relief.

'Come on in, then,' he said, opening his door fully and letting us inside. I liked his room. It was full of pictures of birds, photos and drawings, and with books about birds on the shelves. The drawings were wonderful. He was such a good artist. If we hadn't had other things to do I would have loved to have talked to him about them, told him about the birds on Lindisfarne.

But first things first.

I gave out some Lindisfarne fudge, and then I told them my plan.

'I think I know the story we can tell,' I said.

'What?' said Aidan.

'Our story,' I said. 'We have to tell our own stories, not the stories other people – adults – tell about us. This story started in our school. We have to tell the story of the Quaker boy and the army-family girl, and their families and friends. And how we don't want our school torn apart or newspapers telling lies about us and our families. I still do want to be in cadets, Aidan, but I don't want war in our school. And I don't want your family, or my mum, to be blamed for our school falling apart. So I think our story needs to be about a peace treaty.'

'A peace treaty?' said Nola.

'Yes. I think we need to declare peace and make our school a neutral zone. I want everyone in the school to sign a new petition against having cadets in our school – including you and your parents, Aidan, and me and my grandad – and I want the journalists to be there when we do.'

'You want everyone to sign a petition *against* having cadets in our school?' said Riya. 'But you still want to be a cadet?'

'Yes,' I say.

'I don't understand,' said Nola.

'Neither do I,' said Chloe.

'I definitely still want to be a cadet, but this petition will also ask Grandad and Major Lee to help us start a new detachment in our town, *not* based at the school. Then everyone will be happy. There will be nothing to argue about, and nothing for the newspapers and that horrible MP man to get everyone worked up about.'

'Are you sure?' said Aidan. 'I can't see my parents

being able to sign a petition for a new detachment of army cadets to be started. And your grandad would never agree to abandon the school detachment, surely?'

'I think he would. It all depends on the words we use,' I said. 'If the newspapers can use words to stir things up, we can use words to calm things down.'

'Do you know,' said Grandad, 'I think this is an excellent strategy. A surprise move. Fight fire with fire. I'll sign it myself. We are taking the fight to the enemy, and in this case we are clearly saying that the cadets care more about the community than troublemaking journalists and politicians. It's easier to start a war than broker peace, and I don't like being used by people who care more about their bank balances and shares than their community. No soldier does. Well done, Olivia.'

'I think it is great and I want to help, but I just don't know how we, as Quakers, can ask for any detachment of cadets to be formed,' said Aidan's dad, a bit worriedly.

'We thought of that,' I said. 'The new petition will say that some of the students would like a new detachment of cadets in the town, but, for the sake of peace, the school community as a whole wants any new detachment of cadets to be based, not at the school, but in the town. All the people who sign will not actually be asking for cadets, just saying that *if* there is a new detachment, it should not be based in the school.'

There was a short silence as the adults thought about it.

'That is brilliant!' said Dad. 'Well done, Olivia.'

'I think this could work,' said Aidan's mum.

'We know it will work,' I said.

And it did.

I found out I like organizing things. Grandad came with me to see Mrs Opie and I thought she was very relieved at the compromise, and she said she would back us all the way. She also said she would declare the Monday we come back a day to celebrate peace and suspend normal lessons. I knew that would put everyone in a good mood and give things the best possible start for the healing to begin.

We still didn't have a date for Mum's court case

and the MP, Mr Talbot, was still trying to stir things up against her, but we were determined to get the media involved on our terms. Between us all, we contacted radio and TV stations and as many newspapers as we could, to tell them about our school's plans.

Chloe's mum and dad were brilliant. They went to the school at the weekend, with bunting, and hung it all over the place like there was going to be a celebration. Then, on the Monday when the new petition was announced, Nola's uncle and my grandad came in wearing medals, and Grandad gave a speech to the school about his life in the army and his desire for there to be cadets in the town. But my favourite bit was this bit at the end.

'The Quakers are peacemakers – and the army has a long tradition of peacekeeping. We fight for peace, however much of a contradiction that may seem. I think we can live with the compromise thought up by the students here, and I would like to congratulate my granddaughter, Olivia, who seems to have inherited her mother's love of peace, her father's grasp of peace treaties and her grandmother's need to reconcile people. My grandaughter who, I may add, I am very proud to say still wishes to join the cadets we will be setting up in the town.'

It was perfect. Everyone was so smiley and relieved, and hundreds of students queued up to sign the petition. Not Seb and his friends, but I didn't expect them to, and there was so much noise and colour, and so many of the rest of us, that none of the journalists were interested in interviewing them. We decided to go really overboard celebrating – there were balloons and a big cake with a dove and a Union Jack on, which Chloe's parents brought in – and all this going over the top *worked*.

The newspapers and TV loved the feel-good story. Those of us who wanted to join the cadets talked about how pleased we were that we're going to have a new detachment, and those of us who didn't, like Aidan, talked about how relieved they were it isn't going to be at our school. A big national paper took up the story, and the next day there was a big picture of me and Grandad and Aidan and his parents, smiling with our petition, and a headline that said *Peacemaking and Peacekeeping Runs in Families*. There was a really nice picture of Mum with flowers in her hair as a small inset, and a story about how children in a school had been inspired to make peace. We had interviews on radio and TV, and lots of MPs from different parties came out and said how pleased they were that young people could make peace and come up with a solution when adults couldn't, and how there was hope for the country. One MP even said he thought I should be a politician one day.

Maybe I will be. Doing something – even if it was only getting people to accept that the matter was complicated – was less stressful than not doing anything. Maybe I am more like Mum than I thought.

And at the end of the week, Mum and Sister Mary and Bernard went to court.

Chapter Thirty

Mum and Sister Mary and Bernard went to court and paid their fine. The judge they got was actually very sympathetic and talked about the proud British tradition of conscientious objectors. Mum and Sister Mary and Bernard were interviewed by some national and local newspapers, and on the TV and radio, and everyone was really nice. I think they were still in a good mood after our school event. It all became something to be proud of – they became people to be proud of – eccentric but good British people being decent and honourable and sticking to their principles. It was all so different from what Mr Talbot had tried to make it. He had slunk off and was keeping his head down. Grandad said he doubted he would be voted for again as an MP, that he was an embarrassment to the country. Mum agreed. They agreed a lot, at first. You could tell they were so pleased to be back together in the family. It was a bit of a relief, to be honest, when they started squabbling about gardening and *University Challenge* and cooking again. It was more normal.

Even though she still thought she had done the right thing, poor Mum was a bit shaken up about everything, so in the end she and Johnny decided to take some time out. They had a bit of a holiday in the Lake District, and then Dad helped them find a university course on International Peacemaking and, while they were abroad, studying and working in refugee camps and war zones, he took leave from university and came and lived in London, in Mum's flat, and looked after me there until the end of term. I didn't go back to the vicarage – I stayed with Dad and Stan. I think I will go and live with Gran and Grandad for my GCSEs, but I might even go to sixth form in Durham later. I'd like to spend more time with Dad, and Mum and Johnny are fine about it.

I do really love Mum and Johnny, I've realized. They still drive me mad at times, but I am really proud of them. I don't think I will ever be like them – I am more like Dad – but I am so glad there are people like them in the world. They make the world worth fighting for. Not that they would agree with that way of putting it. But I am talking about the poet William Blake's words in 'Jerusalem' – I am more into 'mental fight'. And I have realized what I really want to be: a historian, like Dad. Seeing all sides of an argument makes me a natural academic, Dad says. And that feels right. But seeing all sides doesn't mean that all sides are equally right – I've discovered that too.

Dad and I went back to Lindisfarne in the summer, and we invited Aidan and his family to come and stay with us and Dad's new girlfriend Alice (who is really nice) in the house Dad's rented again.

Mum bought me a watercolour box for the holiday, and the first morning we were there I decided to get up early and go sketching and painting.

I went on my own, taking Stan with me. I suppose I was secretly hoping we would somehow meet William again.

There was a boy sitting alone on some rocks, sketching. For a moment I thought it was William and my heart lifted. Then I realized that of course it wasn't William at all, just someone who looked a bit like him. Aidan.

Stan pulled so hard I let go of the lead, and he

hurtled his way towards Aidan and jumped up on him, making him drop his sketchbook.

'Sorry!' I shouted.

'Hello, boy!' Aidan said to Stan, making a fuss of him, so that Stan was in heaven. I grabbed Stan and pulled him back.

'I'm so sorry,' I said, my hand on Stan's collar. 'He loves you so much.'

We smiled at each other, and I felt myself blush a bit. Aidan and I were getting on really well. When Dad was staying with me in Mum's flat in term time, Aidan's family often came over for dinner, and we went over to theirs. We met up when Dad came with Grandad and me on birdwatching days, and it had stopped being hard to carry on being friends at school. Everyone knew I was going to cadets and Aidan wasn't, but we still talked to each other and hung out a lot together, and nobody made things difficult. I think everyone had been through so much with all the stuff about cadets, nobody was in the mood to seriously tease anyone about anything for a while. It was restful, but not normal, and I was sure it wouldn't last. To be honest, I knew already I would quite like to be teased about Aidan. And I had the feeling he wouldn't mind being teased about me, if there was something to be teased about. There was plenty of time ahead of us, but I had a feeling our story had only just begun.

Anyway, that morning on Lindisfarne, I didn't let Aidan see that I was a bit disappointed he wasn't William. He wouldn't have understood, of course – what would I have said? 'Sorry, I thought I'd gone back in time again and met a boy who has been dead for years'? I knew it was silly. I knew, deep down, I would never see William again – that we had said all we needed to, and nothing I could have told him from the future would have affected his decision in the past – but I still so wanted to know what had happened to him, and for one moment I had hoped I could see him again and ask.

I smiled while Aidan fussed over Stan.

And then I saw it. William's watercolour box. Beside Aidan on the rocks.

'Where did you get this?' I said. I rushed over, picked it up and stroked it, felt its smooth surface.

'The watercolour box?' said Aidan, looking a bit startled at my reaction to it. 'It was my gran's. It belonged to her dad. He was an artist. He was in the ambulance unit in the First World War, but he got famous afterwards for his paintings of birds. I can show you some at our home, if you like. There are even some in galleries. I never knew him, but my mum says I look like him. I'd really like to be as good a painter as him.'

'What was his name?' I said. But I knew the answer already, and I tried not to show how happy I felt.

'I think he changed his original surname, because his family disowned him when he became a Quaker,' said Aidan. 'So he chose his own. His name was William. The artist William Makepeace.'

Aidan asks me if I would like to go and see William's paintings in a gallery in London with him.

We catch the train together. At first we are a bit shy. It's strange to be alone, without Stan bumping against us and licking us and giving us something to talk about, but very quickly we are laughing and chatting and it is all just normal but exciting at the same time. We are so different, the Quaker boy and the cadet, but we have so much more in common than anything that might divide us.

We walk out of the station and follow our map, and walk into the gallery to find the small room dedicated to William Makepeace.

He came back from the war and he painted birds. Birds of all shapes and sizes; all breeds. Male and female, young and old. He painted birds with black feathers, brown feathers, multicoloured feathers. He painted birds with white feathers. He painted sparrows and birds of prey, doves and seagulls. He loved them all. We walk around the room and see them flying and nesting, swooping and singing and soaring, perching and preening. They dive into stormy waters and rest on calm seas. They swim across oceans, through the air, over land. They cross the divides. They are timeless. They are each different, they are each themselves, they are free, and they are all, and always will be, beautiful.

LETTER FROM THE AUTHOR

Dear Reader

I really hope you enjoyed *Across the Divide*.

I wanted to write a book for children a little like the ones I loved reading so much when I was a child – books about past and present meetings, such as *Charlotte Sometimes* by Penelope Farmer, or *Tom's Midnight Garden* by Philippa Pearce, or *A Traveller in Time* by Alison Uttley. I always found the idea of travelling in time to be so magical!

I also wanted to write something about learning from history, and about listening to each other even when we have different points of view – crossing the divide between 'us' and 'them'. I wanted to write about people who just want to stir up division for their own reasons, and how we can learn to recognise what they are doing and avoid being influenced by them.

I set my story mainly on Holy Island, or

Lindisfarne, a beautiful, ancient island full of wildlife and history, off the Northumbrian coast of England. It is one of my favourite places in the world and somewhere I have visited a lot with my family. We have been there for day trips, but have also stayed in a rented house, similar to the one used by Olivia and her dad.

When the tide is out and the island is not divided from the mainland, there are many interesting things to see and do, but when the daily visitors leave and the tide is in, the place has a particular magical atmosphere. You can walk around parts of the island and, surrounded only by the sea, feel apart from the world and modern times. Looking up at the sky, you are able to catch a glimpse of the same type of birds that a medieval monk or a Viking would have done in their time. It's almost like time travelling!

The castle seems to look down on everything. And the castle is where I learned about Billy Congreve and his story, which was the first inspiration for *Across the Divide*.

The castle was originally built in 1550 and then bought in 1901 by Edward Hudson, the American owner of *Country Life* magazine. Hudson had the castle restored by a famous architect called Edward Lutyens and the garden built by a famous garden designer named Gertrude Jekyll. Today the castle has has been restored to its Edwardian splendour and is owned by the National Trust. You can still go and sit in the garden as Olivia did – it's peaceful, sheltered and quiet and looks exactly the same as it did in Edwardian times.

I am not sure whether Professor Oliver Lodge, who was a real person, ever visited the castle, but I do know that Mr and Mrs Lutyens stayed there, and that Edward Hudson had lots of visitors – he was also engaged to be married to a famous cellist called Madame Suggia. One of his visitors at the castle was a boy called Billy Congreve, who came for two months in 1909 to recover after catching diphtheria, and completely fell in love with the island. Edward Hudson planned to leave the castle to Billy, but the boy grew up to fight in WWI and was killed in 1916 while tending to the wounded under fire.

As soon as I read Billy's sad story, I knew that I wanted to write about a boy staying on Lindisfarne, and then going off to fight in WWI. I started reading about him and other soldiers; I wanted to know why they believed it was right to fight, and also the arguments of those, known as

Conscientious Objectors, who did not feel it was right to fight. The two sides did not understand each other, and many of the newspapers made things worse by telling lies and smearing people as cowards, even though they were bravely trying to follow their consciences.

In my research, I also read about Professor Oliver Lodge, who, like so many parents at the time, was desperately heartbroken after his son was killed during the war. He tried to make contact with his dead son, and some people were shocked when he said that the young man was drinking beer in heaven. I found it very touching that he wanted his son to keep doing his favourite things even after death, so I put that fact in my story and made up the reasons why he might have thought it to be so.

The treatment of Conscientious Objectors during WWI made me think about its relevance today and about the stories we read in our newspapers. I thought about my friends who are peace activists, and about my friends in the army. I thought about children who love army cadets, and I also watched a video by the Quakers against the militarisation of schools. I found an antique watercolour box on eBay. And I wrote *Across the Divide*.

While this book has been going to print, US children have been campaigning to control the sale of guns and to make a change that adults have not managed to achieve. I want all my readers to know that, even as children, you CAN already make the world a better place if you listen to one another's stories, look for the truth, and try to make peace across the divide.

I want you to know that there are other children and adults, now and in history, both real and in fiction, who will stand alongside you in this.

Anne Booth

ACKNOWLEDGEMENTS

I would like to thank the volunteers and staff at The National Trust's Lindisfarne castle, who were very helpful to me when I visited as part of my research, but also on many previous visits, long before I had the idea for the book. Lindisfarne is one of my favourite places to visit.

I would also like to thank Natural England at Lindisfarne National Nature Reserve, who allowed me to join a fascinating walking tour around this beautiful island, and pointed out the extraordinary number of birds to be seen.

In the course of researching this book I have spoken to many lovely people who might be seen as being from across the divide – from high-ranking army officers and a student cadet, to a policeman, and committed pacifists and peace activists. Everyone was very supportive and informative, but not everyone was comfortable about having their name in print, so rather than single anyone out and leave others unacknowledged, I would like to thank them all in general, and leave the individual thanks to when I meet them. Thank you all so much.

I watched online videos promoting army cadets, and also videos by the Quakers against militarisation, and I read newspaper articles about whether we should have cadets in schools.

Amongst the books I read, the following books gave me particular inspiration:

Army Cadet's Pocket Book by Major (Retd) John Hobbis Harris and Elizabeth Rosalie (Davison Military Pocket Books Ltd).

Lindisfarne Castle – an illustrated handbook by The National Trust.

Dear Raymond: The Story of Spirituality and the First World War by Sophie Jackson (Fonthill Media Ltd). This was about Sir Oliver Lodge.

Boy Soldiers of the Great War by Richard Van Emden (Bloomsbury).

Subversive Peacemakers: War-Resistance 1914-1918: An Anglican Perspective by Clive Barrett (James Clarke and Co Ltd).

We will not fight…The Untold Story of World War One's Conscientious Objectors by Will Ellsworth-Jones (Aurum Press Ltd). It had lots about the four Brocklesby brothers, one of whom was a Christian Conscientious Objector, two of whom were soldiers who fought in WW1 and one a recruiting officer. The family supported each other and were not divided, and Phil, one of the soldiers, and Bert, the conscientious objector, were so close that Phil, fighting in France, took time off to visit his brother, in prison in France for refusing to fight.

I was inspired by the words of Dietrich Bonhoeffer, who lived and died in Germany at the time of the Second World War and of Jo Cox, a British MP who worked to heal divisions in the 21st century, and chose to put them at the beginning of the book.

I was moved and inspired by the film Olivia and her father watch, *Testament of Youth*, adapted from the book of that name by Vera Brittain.

I was also lucky enough to find and buy an Edwardian watercolour box, some original copies of *The Western Front* (the newspaper Olivia's dad looks at), and a book by and a contemporary newspaper cutting about Professor Oliver Lodge.

I would like to thank Anne Clark, my agent, Melissa Hyder, my editor, Valentina Vacchelli and Robert Snuggs at Catnip, and all at Bounce marketing, for all their support of *Across the Divide*.

Thank you to the designer Pip Johnson and the illustrator Serena Rocca for a beautiful cover.

Thank you to all my friends who have listened to me talking about this book, particularly Virginia and Ruth. Thank you also to Jonty and Liz.

Thank you, even though they have never read a single book I have written, to my two writing companions, Ben, our spaniel, and Timmy our golden retriever! They often listen patiently to me reading bits aloud, and I appreciate that.

Thank you to my dear school friend Katy and all our English teachers, especially Mrs Igoe, and all my friends and family, off and online, from school days to now, who have encouraged, and do encourage me, in my writing.

And lastly, and definitely not least, thank you above all to my lovely husband Graeme, and our children, Joanna, Michael, Laura and Christina.

Anne Booth lives in Kent with her husband, four teenage children and two dogs. She has worked as a bookseller, a university lecturer and in a care home. She writes fiction for readers aged nine and up about friends, families and the small but significant choices we all face every day, as well as younger fiction for six plus and picture books.

Anne's powerful debut novel *Girl With a White Dog* was published by Catnip in March 2014.

Girl With a White Dog received outstanding reviews and has been nominated and shortlisted for numerous awards including the UKLA Book Award, The Carnegie Medal, The Little Rebels Children's Book Award and the Waterstone's Children's Book Prize 2015.

PRAISE FOR *GIRL WITH A WHITE DOG*

'Jessie is a strong lead character and how she learns about Nazi Germany is turned into an interesting and moving tale'.
THE TELEGRAPH
BEST YA BOOKS OF 2014 SELECTION

'Our heroines (and the reader) are faced with many decisions about their own attitudes to prejudice and their ability to stand up for what they feel is right ... a novel with a powerful punch.'
CLARE MORPURGO
SCHOOL LIBRARIES ASSOCIATION

'It raises issues, challenges prejudice and I know it will stay in my thoughts for a long time ... I loved it and I'd encourage everyone to read it!'
ANNIE EVERALL, CAROUSEL

'A sensitively-told tale, beautifully written.'
MARIE-LOUISE JENSEN, THE HISTORY GIRLS

'This book will change the world.'
RHINO READS

Dog Ears is Anne's second book. This gentle and uplifting story highlights not only the problems faced by young carers, but their invisibility in society.

PRAISE FOR *DOG EARS*

'Well written in a confiding tone, this sad tale tugs at the heart strings.'
JANET FISHER, BOOKS FOR KEEPS

'All in all a beautiful story which highlights in a sensitive and thoughtful way the issues facing young carers across the country. Thoroughly recommended.'
MIDDLE GRADE STRIKES BACK

www.catnippublishing.co.uk
Twitter: @catnipbooks